A retelling of the valiant
fall of England in verse

Hæstingas

JAMES MOFFETT

*To chroniclers of the past
and dreamers of the future.*

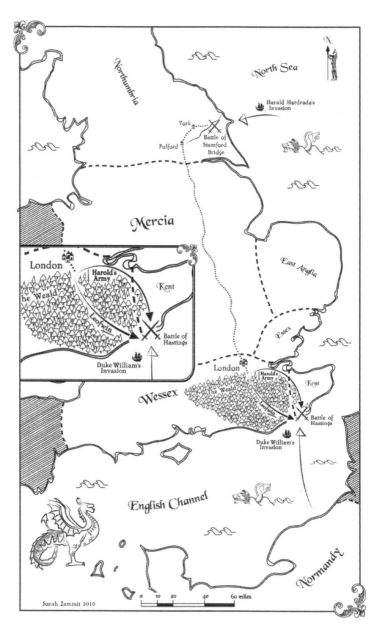

MAP OF ENGLAND, 1066

CONTENTS

Introduction

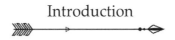

Writing a fantastical tale on the events leading to the battle of Hastings came about through a desire to analyse the balance between myth and historical authenticity.

It will become instantly apparent to the reader that the tale which follows is primarily fictitious — in that certain characters, events, motivations and such narrative expositions, were created for the sole purpose of entertainment rather than as an exploration of the limits of historical accuracy. That is not to say, lest eager historians should be put off by such a claim and discard this book, that this long poem has no references to historical events. Indeed, the key protagonists and occurrences from this particular period in England's history are all to be found in the poem's verses. King Harold, Harald Hardrada, Duke William and others are the basis of this story.

What I set out to do is to experiment with the established accounts and integrate a few ideas of my own — thereby "filling the gaps" as it were, by including a number of fantastical elements to elaborate on the existing literature. Literally, poetic license. As to the decision why such a story needed to be told in verse, the reason was very simple. It was a personal one. I have long enjoyed the great classical epics — *The Odyssey, Beowulf, Paradise Lost*, and *The Divine Comedy*.

It is my belief, however, that the original terminology for the word "epic" has been diluted in everyday language by the rise of digital technologies and the age of social media. A term that was once applied to a piece of visual art or musical composition, has now been assigned to the mundane and the irrelevant. It was therefore my primary intention to attempt to hark back to the classical storytelling style in old myths and tales by constructing a long poem dealing with historical events — conveyed in an elevated style that does justice to the subject matter.

In *Hæstingas*, I set out to reinterpret a piece of history as if written by an 11th century contemporary, attempting to enthral his audience and evoke powerful emotions through the use of verse, imbued with fantastical elements. It should be said that, while I based my approach upon the great works of literature, the poem that follows is written in my own choice of style, rhyming scheme, metre and structure. I sought to craft a poetic piece which ultimately appealed to me.

From the beginning, it was my aim to combine the rhythmic sounds of a ballad, together with the powerful overtones of the heroic epic. For this reason, *Hæstingas* can be best described as a heroic fantasy ballad in iambic tetrameter, or octosyllabic couplets.

Although enamoured by the concepts and conventions introduced in many poetry writings, I found most poetic works to be laborious to read and understand. The flow in many renowned and highly-praised poems felt inconsistent and unnatural to the spoken word, and while this undoubtedly is a subjective interpretation on the part of the reader — and no fault of the poem or poet — I was compelled and determined to present a story of epic proportions that maintained a consistent beat to its verse, whilst flowing naturally from one line or stanza to the next. I was intrigued by the idea of constructing a long narrative that was unambiguous and devoid of the overbearing metaphors, allegories and abstractness that I feel are forced into so many works — especially modern poetry. *Hæstingas* is the kind of poem that could have been sung inside an earl's great hall, and passed down orally through the ages like many of the great classical poems that survived through the tides of time up to the present day.

With reference to the poetic style of *Hæstingas*, there seems to be a rather unfair amount of derision aimed towards the use of octosyllabic couplets. The decision to opt for such style in this work was made purely out of the musicality that came with it. Meanwhile, in an attempt to avoid the oft maligned use of these couple within the narrative — this, in the hope that the repetitive flow of rhythm was broken into episodes. The poem is divided into three sections, with a prologue and an epilogue. It was my intention to structure the narrative in such a way as to clearly delineate the progression and journey of the protagonist and the events as they unfolded.

Throughout this work, a number of verses and words are annotated. These notes appear at the end of this book with explanations and details, together with an index of all the names (characters and objects) appearing in the poem.

The term "Saxon", used throughout the entire work, is a generic reference to the Anglo-Saxon people who settled in England and eventually became known as the English.

Besides the choice of poetic style and the historical subject tackled in this book, it must be impressed once more upon the reader that this poem is a work of fiction — or rather more aptly, fantasy. Although much has been done to base the narrative on the events that took place in those crucial and decisive weeks of 1066, this poem is ultimately a fictional reconstruction.

James Moffett
2019

Prologue

Hush! dear children and mark my song,
where truth sheds lies and right quells wrong.
Listen! and learn from yesteryear
of our cruel foes whom thou now fear.
With Christ's own light of love so pure,   5
thus Heaven-sent this angst does cure.
And with eased heart I now do tell
of such high deeds that once befell.
Such truths spoken in sacred rhyme,
of recent past mislaid by time,   10
loosens my tongue to speak so bold
of tale of worth as yet untold.
Hush now! Beware! the vicious stride
of Norman knight with wasteful pride
that strays too close to this safe den.   15
In Christ our Lord, we trust. Amen!
Come closer now and stay a while
to hear the lay of our own Isle,
where one lone king and warriors brave
fought till the last. Our Home to save.   20
While wicked lords and witches fey
on hapless folk with hate did prey,
do maidens fair and angels bright
fill this long tale with hope and light.

The Hæstingas[1], by God decreed   25
to claim the throne and England lead,
birthed great men whom legends praise
amid heroes of ancient days.
Alas! this land was doomed to fall
under the hoofs of conquest's maul.   30
Its folk now slaves, its pride foregone,
no words uttered of a new dawn.
Yet now do hear how God thus chose
to lead England out of its throes
and bring forth one who sought to shield.   35
his stout people from fate thus sealed.

***

"Hail! Glorious son of Hæstingas.
Declare the tale that comes to pass.
Whereto thou stray on weary ways,
while England's folk whisper thy praise?   40
Upon this road towards the west
to sundered seas, the ever-blessed?
Come! Rest awhile and seek your peace.
Let mortal troubles die and cease.
Come! Heed these words for thine own sake   45
and wash away all grime and ache.
Upon thy brow great sorrow lies —
torment engraved within thine eyes.

Such rumours thrive ere setting sun
of thy prowess in battles won.   50
In undimmed might such songs of praise
the skies will fill till end of days."

On unhelmed[2] face of sweat and gore
a steady gaze and glance he bore.
No proud shield hung by scabbard bare,   55
nor weapon grim that guest did wear.
His battered hands with tattered veins
were drenched with dirt and grisly stains.
Yet that warrior, still and inert,
concealed within some deeper hurt.   60
That lord staggered with wearied will
upon the road where light did spill,
to gaze upon the figure old
who hailed once more with voice so bold:
"Hail! Worthy kin of Hæstingas.   65
Thy armour shines as tarnished glass.
Whereto ride thou as one astray
by failing light at end of day?"

The grassy path that straggler left
and staggered on as one bereft.   70
Towards the wizened speaker went,
sitting beside him as one spent:
"I seek the one who sought me long.
My love, my life, more worth of song."

Thus he declared whose voice did seem   75
as if astir[3] in nightly dream.
That fine warrior in silence sighed —
shorn of honour, deprived of pride.
Ahead he gazed his love to seek
but thereupon began to speak: 80
"Greatest of earls my father claimed.
Briefest of kings my brother famed .
The kindest folk where Angles roam
in fairest land, England my home.
Cursed Leofwin! That is my name,   85
whom folk sing loud and praise its fame.
Loyal in peace, martyr in war.
To safeguard folk I duly swore.
When Wulfnoth Cild, the Saxon thegn,
wrongly accused of crimes in vain   90
by Æthelred[4] the unwise king,
he fled by ship and death did bring.
A son bereft of father's care
still valiant grew, much wise and fair.
Then God decreed Godwin's own fate   95
as loyal liege to Cnut the Great.
The Danish King, pleased by that lord,
gave his servant much-earned reward.
Vast lands he gained and stout strength heaped,
till hearts were stirred by glories reaped.   100
The wise Witan[5] him swift had named
as England's King, and throne soon claimed.

Thus God's warrior in pride arose
to quench and cure his people's woes.
His heirs secured a strong bloodline,   105
and glorious thus the past did shine.
Earl Godwin's sons seven all told:
Old Sweyn the mad, Harold the bold.
Wulfnoth and Gyrth, with Alfgar too,
and that traitor — Tostig untrue.   110
Leofwin too, soon Earl of Kent,
whose young prowess in battle spent.
Then Gunhilda and Edgiva,
daughters were born, with Elgiva;
Edith of Wessex, Edward's[6] Queen,   115
fairest of all that men had seen.
Till Harold throne did then ascend,
and royal line came to swift end."
No more he spoke in stately speech
but gazed at hills beyond his reach,   120
as through that valley blew a breeze
while round those men rustled the trees.

On a sudden the warrior spoke
and up he stood — from slumber woke.
"Hope eternal of England strong,   125
without anguish, without much wrong.
My heart did burn with piety
for peace assured in loyalty.
The King, my kin, I justly served.

The praise I earned was undeserved. 130
For now more worth is her I seek
and without whom my life is bleak.
My heart does crave her warm embrace
and longs to see her graceful face."

Once more silent Leofwin fell 135
and with deep breath his angst did quell,
while the wind mourned for England's fate
and night gathered where shadows wait.

Canto I

As time at end of summer came
there sailed two men with purposed aim.
With turning tides of history
they sought to rid a dynasty.
Two spiders planned for foes to snare   5
as each had claimed their right as heir.
Rumours swept swift of pagan horde
advancing on towards Fulford[1].
The Northern Earls[2] sought to defend
their helpless folk from wicked end.   10
Yet fierce Northmen with raging hate
conquered the land and sealed their fate.

King Hardrada, from Norway came,
to swell his reign and drown in fame.
A cruel tyrant who ruled with sword   15
and tamed the seas with berserk horde.
His great stature dwarfed mighty lords,
and strong-limbed arms tore skulls like cords.
His wicked laugh and roaring cry
filled brave men's hearts with fearful sigh.   20
Him whose subjects praised with great dread,
in strife with Cnut young Harald fled.
Exiled in youth, prowess he earned

as warrior strong, while weakness spurned.
From far-flung East[3] he gained treasures   25
till grown in strength he took measures
to journey back intent on war
against Magnus[4], whose death he swore.
The Danes' marches[5] were soon assailed,
till their king's life thus swift had failed.   30
Such wanton fate had surely sown
Hardrada's claim to Norway's throne.

Now Harald's men through shield walls yelled,
against those Earls[6] who bravely held.
The fields turned red, their foes undone.   35
The Norse conquest had thus begun.
The town was theirs, their pride secure.
Now English throne they set to lure.
As chief of men and warmonger,
of ruthless thirst and vast hunger,   40
with vile Tostig a pact he forged —
that reckless man who on greed gorged.
Earl Godwin's son, wicked and wild,
banished as earl and thus exiled,
with vengeance set through seas he soared   45
to gain England as his reward.
The wind hissed fierce through wizened trees,
while screams chilled hearts and blood did freeze.
The heathen horde unyielding came
unto Jórvik[7], to their next claim.   50

Raven-crested banners and shields.
Odin's rabble beset the fields.
O'er the River[8] triumph assured
as town fell swift and death endured.
Drunk with battle and lust-weary,   55
the Norsemen camped on plains dreary.
At Stamford Bryċg[10] by river blessed,
without a care they laid to rest.
Upon those plains their doom stalked near.
Yet revelry banished their fear.   60
Heedless in hope at subdued foes,
forsaking watch, their fates they chose.

While Harald's men gods' joy had earned,
and sagas sung till their hearts burned,
the Saxon king's own thoughts were blind   65
to Norse raiders who death assigned.
Strained war did brood from Norman land,
as Duke William[10] conquest had planned.
Harold pondered at looming storm
when bearer came, the King to warn.   70
Through doors of court he burst in haste
and on towards his wise sire paced:
"Lord! Look away from southern shores
and punish those who now wage wars.
The Norse king claims the North he owns   75
while Tostig rests on dead men's bones.
The heathen horde your folk now mauls

while life now fails and England falls.
Thy kingdom lies faltering near
to this grave doom of death and fear.   80
More foes will come with each conquest
to stain thy land with blood oppressed.
Shun idleness upon thy throne
and march forth swift to claim thy own.
Lead thy warriors by Jórvik's ruins,   85
and pagans purge of their vile sins.
Save your people from dreadful fate.
Reclaim thy realm ere overlate.
So speaks the tale out of the North.
What say ye lord? Wilt thou set forth?"   90
The enthroned King silent did stare
at southern coast where war lay bare.
The sea breeze howled and keen it roared.
The waves struck minds with fearful chord.

In that high hall of worthy thegns   95
one swift stepped forth with strength in veins,
and there he spoke with burning heart.
With noble voice truth did impart:
"My king, brother, what say thou? Speak!
Godless Norsemen now triumph seek.   100
Tostig our kin betrays us so
and with him leads this cruel woe.
Wilt thou stand firm to face these foes
and banish their abhorrent throes?

Let not our pride so keenly wrought 105
perish fruitless in war unfought.
Wilt thou let men say of our kin,
whose divine blood flows keen within:
'There skulks our King with trembling breath,
who leaves his folk to cruel death.' 110
Deliver not our home England,
as feast for wolves, without a stand.
Shall idleness be thy misdeed
that undoes all the good decreed,
and thy kingdom lies all broken? 115
I, Leofwin, have thus spoken."
His voice was strong, their hearts he stirred.
The dire truth those earls now heard.
He humbly knelt before the King
encircled by that courtly ring. 120
The people loved brave Leofwin —
a Hæstingas, the King's own kin.
With sword prowess and strong-willed mind
his fate was sealed — with doom entwined.

Yet now Harold pondered his pleas 125
and in his heart found much unease.
Then Leofstan, earl to the King,
did speak his mind as doubts did sting:
"O King Harold, do not assent!
Recall to mind that dark portent, 130
ere year had passed when night grew bright

as star traversed and airs did smite[11].
An ill-omen meseemeth clear,
of woes to come by sword and spear.
England will fall if thou march forth   135
to quell attack in untamed North.
Leofwin's words seek needless war
as his parched sword thirsts for fresh gore
on this rabble, this heathen band,
whose feeble raids threaten the land."   140
Young Leofstan thus spoke steadfast.
Such gloom in court his voice did cast.
The King himself silent remained
as words he weighed — by doubts much pained.

Those noble thegns, by angst assailed,   145
their troubled minds deep fears unveiled.
Each one recalled that divine sign
which heralded England's decline.
No thoughts uttered those lords so famed.
The cold court quailed in silence strained.   150
The howling wind in whispers sought
to chill the hearts of all there brought.
Darkly at earl Leofwin gazed,
till once again his own voice raised:
"If northern foes be not opposed   155
England's weakness shall be exposed.
The King must face this heathen threat.
Let Harald's men with swords be met.

To these shores blessed foes will be lured
and our own doom is but assured.   160
Where be now found both sword and shield
of Saxon brave who does not yield?
Where be the strength of England proud
whose sacred folk now lies all cowed?
Let us recall the kings of old   165
and glorious men whose valour told
of daring deeds that did defend
their land and kin from mortal end."
His voice brought hope and warmth to heart,
like arrow swift with hallowed dart.   170
Kindling such strength to thaw chilled soul,
his truthful words minds did console.

The silence reigned in lofty hall
till Harold rose — from slumber tall.
His robes thus shone in dim sunlight.   175
His golden glance, a kingly sight.
"An ill wind blows blasting thus hence,
and sets its will against my sense.
As King I bode much will perish.
O God save us and foes banish!   180
Alas! that this should bear on me,
that I should hear this bearer's plea.
I fear that worse shall come of this
if I set forth and threat dismiss.
Yet words are true and doom now waits   185

through endless leagues at Jórvik's gates.
Let calls be heard, let songs instil.
Set men to march and oaths fulfil."
As Leofwin there pledged his worth,
beside him knelt his brother Gyrth.   190
Before their King they vowed to serve,
the land defend and oaths observe.
The King then gazed upon those two
and down he stepped. Towards them drew.
His hands he placed on their shoulders.   195
Eager he spoke to those young heirs:
"My dear brothers, duty thus calls
on such a quest beyond these walls.
As one we lead our men in war.
Uphold those oaths to me you swore."   200
The two then stood and faced their lord.
Smiling in pride each drew his sword.

Brothers in blood, brothers in bond.
When Rome fell swift[12] their kind had dawned.
Those three brave men, those Hæstingas,   205
above mortals were favoured thus.
A worthy folk — for fame lusted.
Prowess with sword — in God trusted.
That noble kin through humble birth,
though famed in deeds, not thought much worth.   210
From Watt[13] the first of Hæstingas,
England's own kings had brought to pass.

Through that bloodline Godwin soon came.
Earl of Wessex, renowned by name.
Though four daughters and seven sons,   215
only those three were chosen ones.
Thus God did grant to each brother
the gift to wield divine power.
Their swords of fame laid foes to waste.
From relics wrought by the Lord graced.   220

Hammer and thunder the plains shook.
Fierce fire spewed forth from every nook.
The earth rattled. Rumbling, groaning.
The furnace roared. Raging, moaning.
The beating blasts from deep ground swelled.   225
Boiling iron was crushed and quelled.
Sizzling waters spluttered, fizzled,
as Wēland's[14] craft those blades chiselled.
Far underground his smithies roared
while fashioning each Saxon sword.   230
Slender edges and deadly hilt,
golden pommel with runes all gilt.
Forged in secret, in past remote,
while Saint Michael their cores hallowed.
That warrior saint, God's breath breathed   235
upon those swords still unsheathed.
Evil's torment, demon's sore bane.
Kindlers of hope, symbols of reign.
For England's kings as gifts bestowed,

and through their grip mighty strength flowed.   240
Thus Gyrth the young had earned that blade,
Gærscíð[15] by name, whom dark souls preyed.
Keen in battle while swift death wrought
to quench its thirst by blood dear fought.
Leofwin's gift was Fyrecg's[16] bite.   245
Its flaming edge shadows did smite,
while gleaming blade and fine-wrought guard
the stoutest shields with sure stroke marred.
Foreseeing woes in his kingship,
King Harold claimed Nægling's[17] cold grip.   250
An ancient sword whose fierce thrust swayed
the quailing hearts of those who strayed.

Thus Harold, Gyrth and Leofwin,
wove round themselves no armour thin.
Their swords they bore with chivalry   255
o'er dark scarlet, fine livery.
Banners were raised, summons began,
as call spread far among kinsman.
Mercian spearmen keen for great fame,
while loyalists from Wessex came.   260
East Anglia's mercenaries,
beside Kentish dignitaries,
marched eagerly to the King's call.
With lust they sought their foes to maul.
From East Seaxe[18] came those fierce men,   265
devout subjects from field and glen.

These axe wielders had their ranks swelled
by Welsh spearmen whose shafts swift felled.
Relic-bearers brought blessed coffers
with divine gifts of immense powers.   270
While yet more men of Saxons free
came marching in by King's decree.

Amid thousands that gathered there,
a few from Hastings handful were
among King's kin, as their blood bid.   275
Though reticent, true strength they hid.
This band of brothers, bold and true,
of their prowess all men there knew.
Leofwin led these few to war.
No more than twelve to Harold swore.   280
Those Hæstingas rode proudly forth.
From Norsemen's rule to wrest the North,
beside the King and Leofwin
with Gyrth the young among their kin.
Men made ready for brief campaign,   285
to serve and guard their King's just reign.
Brandishing swords, axes and spears
London rejoiced in its folk's cheers.
Crested were shields with proud wyvern[19],
on shoulders borne by men so stern.   290
As the sun dimmed and twilight came
that bold emblem burst all aflame.

The three brothers confession sought,
to purge their sins ere battles fought.
At God's altar they humbly knelt.   295
Bishop Stigand[20] with their souls dealt.
When Leofwin's turn 'twas to tell
to that cleric of what befell,
in honesty thus spoke his mind
with longing heart that made him blind: 300
"Faithful servant to God and King.
My love for both eager does cling.
And Elvyn too, my wife I hold
more dear than life, more worth than gold.
Yet more I feel the need to give   305
to my own home while I yet live.
To England fair much more I owe,
than petty feuds with aimless foe.
Immortal fame I also seek.
The bards to sing, the histories speak,   310
of my own name held in high praise
and glory earn till end of days."

That warrior spoke with fierce fervour,
to reach thus high such endeavour.
To which the Bishop, most perplexed,   315
proclaimed his thoughts in tone much vexed:
"Your uncouth words speak not aloud
for thine own wish is overproud.
Lusting for fame will be thy bane

if thou pursue this worldly gain.   320
Thy desires need more prayers.
Thy ambitions will bring sour tears.
Humble thyself or say farewell
to God's kingdom for endless Hell."
That Saxon lord the chapel left   325
with gnawing doubts and peace bereft.
Yet stubborn pride chilled cautious mind
and blazing heart his wits made blind.

The setting sun soon bowed to night
when early eve brought stars much bright.   330
Silence trembled, the wind thus stirred.
On throbbing airs a din was heard.
The gathered men marched proudly forth
beyond the gates towards the North.
Their ranks flowed swift behind the King,   335
and with stout wills began to sing.
Leofwin forth shieldless thus went,
with sheathed sword and sure intent,
amid his men who cried his name
and beat their shields with swords untame.   340
Yet ere he passed beneath the arch,
a voice rang out that stayed his march:
"Hail Leofwin! Thy swift pace cease.
Take heed! Behold! this wooden piece."
A haggard man with ancient beard   345
amid the crowd thus soon appeared.

With sunken eyes that caught the sun,
he staggered on to Godwin's son.
The Saxon's stride wavered and ceased
as clear voice soared above the feast.   350
That frail old man he soon beheld
whom by Time's hand much years were felled.
The ailing man, in torn clothing,
humbly then knelt and shield did bring
before that lord who urged his guest   355
back to his feet and duly blessed.

"Accept this gift O lord in fear
as thy sore trial swift does stalk near.
In that dour need thou will seek ward[21]
when thine own hands will miss thy sword."   360
The haggard man then raised the shield
for Leofwin to bear and wield.
From alder's bark[22] with cunning wrought,
yet its dark wood no sunlight caught.
A firm iron boss was forged amid.   365
The shield's stout bulk tough strength thus hid.
No gold adorned that barest board
yet battle-scars enriched the ward.
At wooden gift gazed Leofwin.
Unworthy shield for the King's kin.   370
With injured pride anger awoke.
The Saxon lord bitter words spoke:
"Begone beggar! Wilt thou mock me?

I have no need for gifts from thee.
No shield or guard in war I knew.   375
My sword and strength will serve me true.
No need have I to cower blind
behind some scyld[23] of crafted rind.
No helm nor mail shall hinder me
from battle's ire. So begone thee!"   380

The beggar gripped that lord of fame.
To Leofwin whispered his claim:
"Yet bravest men, warriors and lords,
may die perchance by mishap swords.
The unsure flight of a stray dart   385
may pierce bare flesh and stab thy heart.
Count not thy strength alone in war
and see that thee cry boasts no more.
Defend thy soul against thy mind
for vain glory doth make thee blind.   390
More ruinous is your rash pride
than thy worst foes who from thee hide.
Take this with thee, hold back vexed breath,
for wasteful words will be thy death."

Those troubled words Leofwin heard,   395
while in his heart anger swift stirred.
The old man mocked his youthful creed
that warriors bold shieldless could lead.
Still sterner pride grew hot within

21

and grim resolve shook Leofwin.   400
Yet folk rejoiced and praised their lord
who them would save from pagan horde.
With a feigned smile he held his tongue,
while on his back the shield he slung.
Then cries arose among the crowd: 405
"Praise Leofwin! Praise him aloud!"

In concealed shame Leofwin left.
Eager for war, of pride bereft.
Yet ere he joined the Saxons' march,
Elvyn he met beyond gate's arch.   410
He clasped her hands, though cold and bare,
and greeted her with words most fair:
"Farewell my love, I ride away.
I leave our home as world turns grey.
Though journey North may end awry,   415
my love for you shall never die.
Pray for my soul not my disgrace
that I may thee once more embrace.
Glories untold I shall thus reap
and in my heart thou will I keep.   420
I pray to God for my return
yet till that day for thee I'll yearn."
That lady's smile broke men's sternness,
as down she looked in her kindness:
"Farewell my lord in such dark days.   425
No need have I for battle's praise.

22

Yet thine own self do safely keep,
and until then my heart shall weep."
Her golden hair untied blew free
as icy wind swept from the sea.   430
In silence stood those two in grief,
as sun westered[24] in moment brief.

Throughout the land horn calls echoed.
The King set forth upon the road.
Elvyn shuddered at horses' shrieks,   435
while tears fell down her scarlet cheeks.
A parting kiss he gave his bride,
and 'neath stern face his heart thus cried.

***

And thus it was late summer's eve.
September's frost began to cleave   440
when Leofwin, with his brothers,
rode North to face those invaders.
Tireless marched those housecarls bold,
brave royal men from King's household.
Ranks of fyrdmen[25] to Harold true —   445
to what sure end none there then knew.
Through wooded roads that scarlet trail
of Saxons moved in nightly veil.
To Jórvik led the long road clear,
amid the fields of land so dear.   450

Upon the road they met the call
of fleeing men from Fulford's fall.
With rusted swords and stained mail rent,
came the Earls's troops much hurt and spent.
"My King!" they cried, "alas such dread!   455
With battle doomed from fields we fled.
Upon this road sure doom awaits.
Turn back thy host to London's gates.
The North is lost, our foe has come
and with swift strides much will succumb.   460
They surge like gods from distant lands
and strike our folk with mighty hands."

The King rebuked Earl Morcar's act
to leave his kin as town was sacked.
In wrath he turned on Eadwine too   465
and bitter words towards him threw:
"Disgraced warriors! Unworthy fools!
How dare you flee O craven ghouls.
From our own folk you swore to guard,
though death be swift and land be scarred!   470
Redeem God's grace and march along
towards the North, and right your wrong.
We ride to face this horde from hell
and with sharp swords their ills expel."

That Saxon host its ranks now swelled   475
with those shamed men who their prides felled.

Through wind-swept glens their quest now led
where silence grew and unease spread.

Canto II

Greatest of feats ever decreed,
we praise in awe King Harold's deed.
Ere sun had soared on the fifth day,
his banners rose at sight of prey.
Though cloudless sky land did adorn   5
a cloudy veil appeared in scorn.
The light was dim, a stench arose,
and over plains there loomed shadows.
Soon Harold's host from hill did gaze
towards the east beyond the haze.   10
The land sloped down to Jórvik's town,
with gates broken and walls thrown down.

As strong winds blew from ruthless seas,
there rose a cry of people's pleas
as dismayed folk faced their sure doom.   15
Laments rose high with burning plume.
Pity and rage stirred in King's eyes
while wind blew keen those forlorn cries.
His mourning men forward stumbled
while Leofwin his wrath kindled.   20
Restless they stood hoping to heed
the cry to charge and their foes bleed.
Yet day wore on without the call

for men to cause Hardrada's fall.
Silent on horse Leofwin scowled   25
at deep scorched earth and peace befouled.
He spurred his steed in angered mood,
roaring at men while unrest brewed:
"Behold! our foes who blood have shed,
and with their swords the lands have fed.   30
In bitterness shall England rue
if the Norse king's own wish comes true.
Listen my King! to thy folk's woes
while their shrill cries reveal grim throes.
Wilt thou ponder thy rightful course,   35
while land is lost to heathen force?
Tarry no more on stale counsel,
but urge thy men — their thirst instil.
Lead thus the way and swift assail
the encamped host beyond this vale.   40
There lies Tostig with the Norse king,
and ere night falls of their deaths sing."

Yet King Harold in silence gazed,
staring eastwards till eyes he raised.
On horse rose he and backwards glanced   45
while loud he cried in voice entranced:
"Sons of England! To call hearken!
Beset thy foes as skies darken.
Alight your steeds and wield the sword.
Follow your King and rout that horde!"   50

27

Horns eager sang. The signal blared.
Harold on foot the fields now dared.
Behind him leapt eight thousand men —
in silence stalked upon the fen.
True Leofwin came on his right,   55
Gyrth to his left — eager for fight.
Jórvik's ruins with care they reached.
Thousands poured through the walls now breached.
Sinister voices of the dead
seemed to follow the Saxons' tread.   60
Stillness settled in barren town
as burning homes rife cries did drown.
Yet hope there sprung in sullen airs
amid the reek of painful tears.
Whispers spread far of King returned,   65
as mournful cries for Harold yearned.
Leofwin led his men ahead,
before the King they stalked the dead.
With swords wielded and shields unslung,
for fierce battle their hopes had sprung.   70
Behind them poured Harold's thousands.
Axes and spears in their grim hands.
With care they moved amid the town,
as golden sun by smoke turned brown.
Upon the slain all faces fell.   75
For butchered folk their hearts did swell.
Men and women, their deaths contrived,
and fair children of life deprived.

Once through the eastern gates they passed,
the Norse raiders they saw at last.   80
While the smoke cleared and plains exposed,
those cursed heathens were unopposed.
The few townsfolk who death survived,
of their freedom they were deprived.
And though they begged, their lives were felled   85
while others more as slaves were held.
Yet as Norsemen descried their foe
more blood they spilt o'er fields of woe.

Those Saxons grim looked on in grief
as their slain folk brought no relief.   90
Then Gyrth in madness broke his shield
and with both hands his sword did wield.
The foremost twelve with Leofwin
roared in anger at fallen kin.
"Heathens beware! Thy doom is bleak.   95
Brothers! Strike down and vengeance seek."
Thus Leofwin did cry aloud
before whose voice the Norsemen cowed.
Onwards they charged with fiery eyes.
England's warriors with mighty cries.   100
All twelve of them, the Hæstingas,
their stomps dug deep upon scorched grass.
And thereupon Harald's vanguard
faltered in grit[1] — their joys now scarred.
The Saxons' rage that contest won   105

29

as helpless foe soon turned to run.
Norse deaths dealt swift as blood was spilled.
The grassy plains with corpses filled.
Leofwin's sword was deftly swung.
All those before him down he flung.   110
As clash of battle soon died down
King Harold passed beyond the town.
His host followed and all beheld
hundreds of Norsemen fiercely felled.
There Harold saw his brothers bent   115
on swords leaning, their fervour spent.
Amid those men, all soaked in gore,
their breath was deep yet strength still bore.
"The Lord's favour on you does rest
as your own strength this war will test."   120
Thus Harold said striding ahead
towards his kin, with helmets shed.
"Yet Norse king lies beyond these plains
for his main host still strong remains.
Let us make haste and tarry not.   125
We march at once to foe unfought."

As day wore on, with march still long,
they burst into a mighty song.
In God's favour their spirits soared
while voices rang praising the Lord.   130
Towards the east more miles they trudged
till a faint glean ahead they judged.

Beyond a wooded ridge there flowed
a river strong cleaving the road.
The Derwent roared and sunlight caught.   135
A chill drizzle to men soon brought.
A single wooden bridge there spanned
where only three abreast could stand.
Ere long the King with his host gained
its foamy banks where waters drained.   140

A lone horn rang across the land
which shook the heart of conquest planned.
Through the crisp air that call quivered
beyond where water keen slithered.
There Harald stood stricken by fear   145
yet unaware of foe so near.
Cold dread soon spread on eastern side[2]
as half-waked men, drunken by pride,
cried in dismay as there appeared
the Saxon host. Their swords they feared.   150
As if by spell or evil craft
in mockery their gods thus laughed.
In their folly they never thought
to keep a watch while ransack sought.

While Norsemen fled in disarray,   155
Saxons did thirst to join the fray.
To cross the bridge was King's intent,
and shield wall form whilst forward went.

Amid men's screams shouting *Backward!*
a lonely warrior cried *Forward!*   160
Frenzied he ran towards the west.
On bridge he stood — triumph to wrest.
Bereft of helm or firm armour,
through bearded mouth he roared anger.
The Norse berserker held his ground   165
as mighty axe he swung around.
A few Saxons, glory lusting,
thus rushed ahead in strength trusting.
To overthrow the giantling[3]
the archéd path they reached yearning.   170
In one fell swoop all heads tumbled.
King Harold's men their pride humbled.
The wooden bridge turned vile crimson.
The whole army was grief-stricken.
The Northman's fury shook the earth   175
while bloodied axe he swung in mirth.
Standing firmly to weapon clung,
from raging eyes men's downfall sprung.

"Stay your madness!" Harold thus yelled,
as path ahead against him held.   180
Yet more brave men dared disobey,
to cross the bridge and clear the way.
The Nordic axe at armour hacked.
The river flowed with corpses stacked.
As sun rose higher time was lost   185

yet blood-soaked bridge remained uncrossed.
Hardrada grinned at Harold's plight,
as loss of men did please his sight.

While English fey[4] were held at bay,
his host rallied — fortune to sway.   190
The heathen king his men did dread,
With firm grip ruled and terror fed.
With thick forked beard and long-curled hair,
his bright cold eyes none dared long stare.
On warhorse sat his robust frame   195
though eight feet tall rumours did claim.
A dark blue cloak fluttered behind,
while his bare strength in mail confined.
Beside him stood Frírek the Bold.
The king's standard aloft did hold.   200
That immense flag was thus adorned
with dark raven — by rivals scorned.
The Landøyðan[5] in fear renowned.
Prophecies claimed it ever crowned
as sole victors those who thus bore   205
before their hosts that flag to war.
Its mighty beam loud creaked and groaned.
The foul raven shrill croaked and moaned.
That grave portend now wild fluttered,
as Saxons grim gazed and shuddered.   210
A strong shield wall assembled swift,
a solid bulk without clear rift.

Behind it stood the Norse king stern
as war-cries rose, his foes to spurn.
Harold's own line in turn restless,   215
their wrath hindered from sweet redress.
From eastern bank those Norsemen jeered.
With lust for blood their faces smeared.
The berserker still firmly stood.
With wild frenzy he struck the wood   220
to crush the bridge and halt advance.
Such task he took with stubborn stance.

Impatient Gyrth reached for his blade.
Yet ere he drew his hand was stayed.
For Leofwin ahead thus stepped   225
and far from them he swiftly leapt.
Towards the giantling he sped
with sword in hand, no helm on head.
A cry soared high from fierce warrior.
Leowfin bold. England's saviour.   230

"Stay brother! By King's decree!
To death shall lead thy own folly!"
The ground shook fierce from King's rare ire
though bridge to gain his need was dire.
Of lord heedless was Leofwin.   235
With divine blood pulsing within,
he rushed upon the guardian
knowing no fear, that champion.

With arms outstretched he challenged him
whilst world turned grey as sun soared dim.   240
That guardian cried, to gods he preached.
Then God's warrior the bridge soon reached.
The Norseman sneered. His heart did leap.
His axe he raised with force to sweep.
Leofwin jumped and through the air   245
brandished his sword — at soul to tear.
The berserker swiftly stepped back.
The Hæstingas his aim did lack,
for mighty sword struck wooden planks
with godly strength that broke the banks.   250
The brute kicked hard his rival's breast
and pushed him back to pierce his chest.
Yet Leofwin in haste had turned,
swerving aside and clear sight earned.

His sword he swung with vicious force.   255
Keen iron hacked flesh off that Norse.
The axe fell down with heavy thud,
from severed arm gushed forth much blood.
Hardrada's man screamed in anguish.
Leofwin grinned at fulfilled wish.   260
With one bold thrust he drove his blade
through Norseman's heart till soul did fade.

Once bridge was won and guardian slain,
with King Harold many a thegn

the river crossed to form a wall   265
of stubborn shields and their foes maul.
As both armies each other faced
their shields held firm, for battle braced.
Swords gripped tightly, spears thrust forward,
yet no horn blew nor call they heard.   270
In staunch resolve two bulwarks kneeled.
Fierce eyes now leered between each shield.

Wicked Norseman eyed Saxon brave.
Their foe's frail souls they would deprave.
Odin's ravens lusted to slay   275
Wessex's wyvern ere close of day.
Bold Leofwin Tostig now sought —
that vile traitor who woes had brought.

As the wind blew and smoke did rent
above the roar of the Derwent,   280
there rose a noise of men marching —
horn calls sounding, armies startling.
From Ricall[6] came thousands in haste,
behind Norse shields they now thus paced.
Hardrada's force swelled thick and vast.   285
Barbarian ranks were soon amassed.
With them were those who far north dwell.
From Orkney's isles joined men much fell.
The Earl brothers, Paul and Erlend[7],
thus craved in thought rule to extend.   290

Amongst them rode a lone rider
who plots had schemed — that young spider.
With that traitor's wicked sneer spurred,
had England's woes been sourly stirred.
"Lord Tostig comes!" those Norsemen cheered,   300
with joy upon their faces smeared.
A force of Scots with him had brought,
and allegiance with Flanders wrought.
Hardrada's ranks in haste bolstered.
Yet brave Saxons were not deterred.   305
Both connivers each other hailed.
On horses sat, their plans unveiled.
It now was clear how Tostig held
his rightful place in ploys impelled.
King Edward's death had left the throne   310
for unjust claim — kingship to own.

While both armies did not engage,
Leofwin's wrath once more did rage
as he descried his own brother
grinning in sin of a traitor.   315
From wall broke he — at foe to get.
Towards Tostig his gaze was set.
The twelve Hæstingas at his back.
While Gyrth the young no urge did lack.
Thus Leofwin, his sword held high,   320
jumped over shields with mighty cry.
Heedless of hurt the lines he broke

of steadfast men with sure death stroke.

The Hæstingas their skill displayed.
As battle joined to God they prayed.   325
The screams of dying foes did fill
that field where misery rose shrill.
Leofwin's sword burst all aflame —
that renowned blade, Fyrecg its name.
Those Englishmen God's sign beheld.   330
Their shield wall broke whilst *Charge!* they yelled.
In firm gripped hands their swords waving.
On rounded shields men's spears thrusting.

The Saxons clashed and hacked and clove,
and through the Norsemen sweeping drove.   335
The two forces fought furiously.
Both sides' prowess earned gloriously.
The onslaught raged till sun westered,
as will thus waned and wounds festered.
Like demons screamed the hordes from hell.   340
As heathens suffered, swift they fell.
The battered Hæstingas bellowed.
Amid the clash war-cries echoed.

No mortal eyes had yet beheld
how feeble Man his own kin felled.   345
With savagery was world shaken,
as endless lives were swift taken.

Like roaring waves in fierce tempest,
each Saxon crashed his shielded breast.
The din of battle thundering.   350
The screams of slaughter deafening.
The three brothers of worthy fame
with skill wielded their swords aflame.
Standing within a fiery storm
they held at bay the raging swarm.   355
Such divine fury they harnessed,
the King and kin whom God had blessed.
With flaming swords their foes they purged
as bloodied blades flickered and surged.
The Hæstingas around them stood,   360
as any faithful subject should.
Amid the fray, housecarl and thegn
for England cried — Heaven to gain.
With shields they pushed and swords they hacked,
whilst spears they thrust as shield wall cracked.   365
The heathens cursed as their strength waned
and ground was lost while Norse blood drained.
Leofwin's strength, surging anew,
in a firm leap his whole frame threw,
and breaking through the Norsemen's wall   370
the Saxons rallied to his call.
Shields did collapse at his dared dash.
With one sword's thrust there rose a crash.
A mighty wind soared through the air.
Plucking up men, their lives did tear.   375

A force unseen blew foes like hay.
God's breath emerged from sword to slay
and bring an end to unjust raid
ere all else fail should England fade.
Thereupon the Norsemen faltered. 380
To face King's kin none there had dared.
Yet onwards came the Saxons stout,
while staunch Norse ranks turned to a rout.

As Harold's troops slaughter began,
the King's brother descried a man — 385
that naysayer who professed doom
among the thegns in courtly gloom:
"Onwards Saxon! Before thee lie
thy pagan foes who flee to die.
Thy King's decree do not now shun, 390
and let all mark brave Leofstan!"
Thus Leofwin, with battle lust,
that warrior mocked and forward thrust.
A frenzied mood of joy and zeal
the Saxon lord's drained limbs did heal. 395

Arrows flew fierce in that foray
that one lone shaft sharp fled astray.
From Norseman's bow, in deadly flight,
it pierced the air yearning to smite.
At Leofwin it aimed its thorn, 400
while he heedless — of armour shorn —

bound in bloodshed he missed the dart
while fate kept it far from his heart.
His back he turned blindly away,
and the fixed shield it struck like prey.   405
The shaft quivered in wooden guard
and no frail flesh it clove or scarred.
Leofwin laughed at such blessing
and God he thanked, his praise did sing.
Unto young Gyrth he called out loud   410
with steadfast voice and will uncowed[8]:
"It would have pleased that old man's heart
to hear the tale of this wild dart,
knowing his shield had served its use
and my own life from death did loose."   415
He swung and stabbed and Norsemen slew,
while Harold's brave ruthless did hew.
The air grew hot, the fields turned red,
while cries soared high and notched swords bled.

Ere all was lost and doom assured,   420
Hardrada came while host endured.
Raging in wrath, aloft he bore
a mighty hammer famed in war.
Endless the drums did beat and roar,
deep underground on anvil's core.   425
Pure ore was dug and with skill forged
in furnaces that on coal gorged.
The dwarf blacksmiths so long had wrought

the king's hammer which he now brought.

With Harald came Tostig sneering,   430
with axe and shield, naught else fearing.
Flemish allies and Scots he led,
joining the fray where dread they spread.
The Landøyðan hearts did uplift,
urging men back and foes seek swift.   435
Those fleeing souls with hearts inflamed
took up their arms and charged unshamed[9].
This twist of fate brought sudden lust
as pagan horde, with renewed trust,
returned to fight by their king's side   440
and those great earls who turned the tide.

Among Harald's best warriors came
Eystein Orre[10] of noble fame.
Finest of friends in the king's guard.
His battle axe Saxon thegns scarred.   445
Beside the king he deftly swung
his great weapon and heads he flung.
Hardrada waved his war hammer
amid the battle's harsh clamour.
The earth did shake when ground it struck   450
and scattered dust with bloodied muck.
"Bring me the head of Godwin's son!
ere this battle is quelled and won.
If none now here their king will heed,

I'll claim myself such high a deed!"   455
At Saxon King he went in rage,
to slay Harold and wrath assuage.
He swept aside those housecarls brave
who for the King their lives they gave.
The hammer struck and King's shield bent.   460
Down succumbed he with strength much spent.
Hardrada swung such fearsome blows
on groaning King weakened by throes.
Three times he struck Harold's firm shield
as it withered while bearer keeled.   465

"Yield! and renounce England's frail throne.
Declare thy realm to be my own.
Kneel! to Odin and thou shalt plead,
ere my hammer on thy blood feed.
Kneel! For your life is at an end   470
and swift to Hel[11] thou shalt descend."
The King's body with each strike shook.
As hammer fell his strength it took.
Lower he sank on muddy field
as the last blow broke through his shield.   475
Harold fell down with arm injured.
His sword he lost. From fight hindered.
The Saxons quailed at their King's plight
as Norse king lunged to end the fight.
Leofwin gazed with much distress.   480
To aid Harold he was helpless.

Urged into fray by Tostig's force,
he battled through many a Norse.
Those two brothers, bonded in blood,
fiercely did clash whilst churning mud.   485
Tostig, vicious in treachery,
showed much prowess and bravery.

Meanwhile Harold across the field
lay on the ground bereft of shield.
Hardrada loomed with both hands raised   490
and hammer swung while Odin praised.
The Saxon King for death readied.
His foe he faced and heart steadied.
As Norse king roared, for blood lusting,
he dealt a stroke in strength trusting.   495

Ere hammer crushed King Harold's head
Hardrada's arms faltered and bled.
Gyrth's fiery sword he brought to bear
on assailant as flesh did tear.
As Hardrada backwards staggered,   500
such hideous cry both armies heard.
In his own blood the hammer drenched,
yet in his hands was firmly clenched.
Plunging forward to shield the King,
light-footed Gyrth his sword did swing.   505
At Norse king drove his fervent blade
though his great foe was not dismayed.

Back to his feet Hardrada rose
and parried off each blow swung close.
He grinned eager at that young prey   510
as if he faced some child at play.

"Valhalla!"[12] cried those heathens cursed.
Through Saxon shields they staunchly burst
as back they rushed with renewed lust.
In their false gods they put their trust.   515
Leofwin's flank was still oppressed
as Tostig's men their tough shields pressed.
Weakened, Harold's men forward urged
as foes rallied, forces emerged.
The Saxon army ground had gained   520
though shields crumbled and earth was stained.

Towards the coast they pushed their foes
while revelling in their death throes.
War-wearied Gyrth gave one last thrust.
Keenly he clove, for blood did lust.   525
His sword drove through Hardrada's knee
and, dragged back swift, the blade was free.
A crimson stain smeared the king's limb
as he fell down and sight went dim.
Yet Gyrth's glory thus soon faded,   530
as Harald[13] rose with surged hatred.
He towered over Gyrth's small frame.
Gritting his teeth he now was lame.

He brought the hammer crashing down
and Gyrth's frail skull in blood did drown.   535
No scream escaped, no cry of pain
did that young lord utter in vain.
His body fell as one unworth[14]
while sword sank deep in mud-soaked earth.

Those Hæstingas and Saxons near,   540
heedless of war, wavered in fear.
Bitter they wailed at unjust death
of their fair prince bereft of breath.
Hardrada urged his men to fight
as England reeled from ghastly plight.   545
Harold staggered towards his kin,
grim in despair and grief-stricken.
He knelt beside Gyrth's lifeless youth,
removing helm and sword in ruth[15].
He cared no more for cruel war   550
and in anguish his beard he tore.
Leofwin saw what there befell
and broke thus free from that stunned spell.
Fury took him to the world's end
as men rallied — King to defend.   555

Hardrada swept through the King's guard.
Hammer brandished, countless skulls marred.
His wide-eyed stare none could defy
and many there were doomed to die.

"Protect the King!" Leofwin cried 560
as his men pushed Tostig aside.
Once more unto the breach they rushed.
Foe against foe, each other crushed.
Harald, in mirth, their deaths he mocked.
Through crowded fray Leofwin stalked. 565
He slew all those who barred his way
and advanced forth towards his prey.
The Hæstingas rushed round their King,
kneeling steadfast to form a ring
of shields and spears locked side by side 570
amid bloodshed at turn of tide.

The high sun soon traversed the sky
towards the west as eve was nigh.
Yet fight raged on with no victor.
Each side called men — triumph to spur. 575
Leofwin lunged at the Norse king,
raising his sword ready to swing.
In both their stares there strove a will
of sure resolve, his foe to kill.
"Craven beggar! Before me plead, 580
by flaming sword thou swift shall bleed
for ruin wrought on fair England
betwixt Tostig, whom death had planned.
Not least my brother, my own kin.
Bitter shall thou pay for thy sin. 585
On blood in glee I feast tonight

once thee I slay at end of fight."
Leofwin's voice in great anger
spat high above the fierce clamour.

Deftly he fought with skill unmatched.   590
The fight's favour he soon had snatched.
Hardrada's blows, though vile as Hell,
his skilled rival he failed to fell.
Leofwin's sword, once more inflamed,
struck Harald's cheek and his eye claimed.   595
That king staggered and loud he howled,
while in torment his head he bowed.
Through bloodied eye back up he gazed
at Godwin's son and hammer raised.
Dashing forward he sprung up high   600
wading the airs, and with a cry
came crashing down amid the fray
to wreak havoc amongst his prey.
As hammer smashed, like a frail thing,
the earth collapsed to form a ring.   605
A wild wind flung both friend and foe,
with violence strewn by the blow.

In that grim hour a silence reigned
as if the world a doom proclaimed.
No man was struck as strife faltered,   610
and thoughts then spread of fates altered.
The earth did shake from the king's smite.

Through weapon fierce coursed such dark light,
and there arose thick wisps of smoke
high up above the sky to choke.   615
The dark cloud turned into a shape
and coiled itself with jaws agape.
Till from the plume flew swiftly forth
a great fýrdraca[16] of the North.
Its fiery eyes on hornéd head   620
struck every man with mortal dread.
Its wingspan tore at darkened cloud
as down it came roaring aloud.
The dark-hued scales of the winged beast
did glow alight, while to the east   625
it flew in ire and wild flames spewed
on the Saxons — their strength subdued.
Men were smouldered upon scorched earth.
In storm of fire the field was girth.

Thus the dragon conquered the skies,   630
as a sure doom to mortal eyes.
"Starkheart![17] The scourge of Christians' faith,
by Odin's will unleash your hate."
Thus Harald's cry once more did urge
his host to charge and with fire purge.   635
The Saxon wall was soon shattered
as raven-crested shields battered.
The ranks of men broke swift and fled.
Back to the bridge their paths thus led.

Only Harold lay there silent,   640
with Gyrth now dead, his body bent.
Surrounded by the Hæstingas,
still kneeling firm upon the grass.

As Starkheart relished in retreat,
hunting for sport and for fresh meat,   645
he plucked up men in mighty jaws
and tore through flesh with sharpened claws.
Over the bridge the dragon flew
sending forth blasts and Saxons slew.
Both earth and air turned ashen grey   650
as the creature their skins did flay.
Meanwhile, in joy at victory
Hardrada revelled in glory.
While false Tostig his horde rallied,
to the Derwent their flags carried.   655
In cutting off the Saxon's flight
the dragon perched on bridge in might
with its clawed legs all four resting
on weakened wood — its strength testing.
The fierce flutter of Starkheart's wings   660
sent forth a reek that plagued all things.
An evil gust of wind beset
that Saxon force as end there met.
As between hammer and anvil,
the Saxons thus lost all their will.   665
From east and west no hope was paved

for England free nor their lives saved.
Yet Leofwin once more ran east
towards his foe like a wild beast.

The vanguard struck and lives banished.   670
Fyrecg his sword with skill brandished.
While his men fled in disarray,
and pagan horde hindered his way,
Leofwin ran back to the King
among the Hæstingas's bold ring.   675
There to die in high honour
amongst his kin and praise garner.
Perhaps he hoped at last to slay
Tostig the false ere end of day.
Behind those shields steadfast were bound   680
those few crouched men holding their ground,
while all the rest fled Harald's ire
only to meet the dragon's fire.
As foes approached Leofwin saw
a relic bearer who close did draw   685
towards his chest a coffer small
while on the grass in fear did crawl:
"Craven Hrodulf! Stand your ground man!"
Leofwin roared while to him ran.
Ere Norsemen joined once more the fray   690
that zealot shook with wild dismay.
"Stay your angst and yield the relic!"
Leofwin urged that scared cleric.

Coffer he grasped with fervent will
while bearer urged whose heart was chill. 695
Towards the Hæstingas they went
as Hrodulf fell beside King spent.
Leofwin stood before his kin,
his mouth shaping into a grin.
As Norse warriors eager soon reached 700
that feeble shield wall not yet breached,
the Norse king limped — for blood did thirst,
while drained Tostig by his side cursed.

Bloodied hammer aloft he swung
and cried aloud in his own tongue. 705
Through storm of wind the dragon soared
to its master, its overlord.
Thus bridge was clear for Saxons' rout —
yet as their dread turned into doubt
they saw their lords alone steadfast 710
against the beast and hordes amassed.
Many then ran back to their King,
shamed by their flight — their fears facing.
Their shields they grasped, swords repossessed,
and thus their cowardice redressed. 715
Planting their shields a wedge they formed.
Behind the King they knelt and swarmed.
"Hail to the King graced by Our Lord!"
all those Saxons cried in accord.
Their voices rang upon the plain 720

and shook the air as strength did gain.
That pagan horde's vicious assault
faltered and came to sudden halt.

Yet Harold lay oblivious.
To rife turmoil, impervious.   725
Still Leofwin's resolve hardened
as from the West blew a fresh wind.
With coffer cracked, inside it lay
a small phial with crimson ray.
A clear droplet of blood encased   730
and in both hands the glass he placed.
His eyes he closed and relic raised
as sunlight through it bright thus blazed.
Behind him kneeled all that remained
of Saxon host as grit regained.   735
Leofwin prayed, softly he spoke,
then crushed the glass and phial he broke.

From hands emerged a trail of white,
basking aglow in pure bright light.
Godwin's own son kneeled fore the Flame —   740
drifting gently with purposed aim.
Upon the sign of the cross made,
so too his kin while kneeling stayed,
the Flame burst forth with radiance pure.
All weariness there then did cure.   745
Even Harold from grief was healed.

Lighter of heart, his senses reeled.

Beyond the glow Harald doubted.

In fear his men curses shouted.

The dragon roared and thus defied   750

the radiant orb with bestial pride.

"Some trickery of their own god!"

Hardrada cried — in secret awed.

Tostig doubted that blinding light,

yet urged men forth into the fight.   755

The Saxon host, in silence graced,

their foes beheld — for battle braced.

From Haestingas light ascended

and with the Flame swift thus blended.

Akin in sight to divine sun,   760

that ball of light pulsating spun

towards the gloom of the dark cloud

as the dragon again roared loud.

A humble knight on pale horse reared

before their eyes there soon appeared;   765

amid the Flame so pure and bright

as it rose up to soaring height.

That divine blood and vision bright

belonged to him who once did fight

with Rome's legions, victorious.   770

A humble man was Georgius[18].

By Christian faith he lived hard days

as he refused false gods to praise.
To death condemned for this resolve,
though by God's grace was soul absolved.   775

The divine knight now held his lance.
Grasping the reins forth did advance.
At the dragon he rode in haste
as searing Flame at darkness raced.
While both spirits soared through the skies,   780
those mortals clashed with fervent cries,
as each rival sought to regain
triumph assured from their foe's slain.
The Saint's lance smashed through dragon's hide.
In radiant light they did collide.   785
Those two titans, their strength immense,
thus shook the world in violence.

Never before was ever seen,
nor ever will such conflict keen.
A mighty duel burned the sky   790
as the world's end came almost nigh.
Fire rained fierce on battlefield.
No Norse or Saxon would now yield.
Lightning blinded, thunder deafened.
Blows were still struck and lives lessened.   795
Leofwin faced Tostig once more.
Their armour rent covered in gore.

Beside them fought Harold returned.
The Saxon king vengeance thus yearned.
King Hardrada he faced anew. 800
Despite his wounds, the Norse king drew
much strength of will to threaten death
and earn triumph ere his last breath.
And yet it was in fated hour
victory's taste swift turned so sour. 805
Tostig was struck with flaming blade.
Treason in blood was duly paid.
Though much wearied and strength waning,
Leofwin held — his will straining.
Forcing himself in thickest fray 810
cutting down foes — leading the way.
Harold's own grief he soon mastered
as renewed strength coursed unhindered,
through weary limbs and heavy heart
agile and deadly as a dart. 815
Till finally his sword he drove
through Harald's chest and heart he clove.

The hammer fell from Norse king's grasp
as blood gushed forth with his last gasp.
As Hardrada fell without life, 820
in Norse army terror was rife.
The king was dead, their wills broken.
And so they fled, their prides stolen.
Yet some Norsemen frenzied by fear,

wild in berserk, charged from the rear.   825

In bloodlust roared to seek their foes
and deal much death in grim shadows.
Among them was noble Eystein.
The Landøyðan he bore in line.
Into the fray Saxons beset,   830
till his own death weakened their threat.

Lusting for blood Leofwin led
the onslaught fierce as horror spread.
The Saxons followed him in glee
driving their foes towards the sea.   840
Meanwhile the Saint his lance had thrust
through dragon's heart which turned to dust.
The winged beast roared in such torment
till it perished, its spirit spent.
Men raised their hands in wild prayer   845
for divine knight — the wyrm[19] slayer.

As they rejoiced and him did praise,
the sun let out its lasting rays.
Before their eyes the knight faded
into a haze of mist sacred.   850
And thereupon Leofwin sighed,
with strength battered as fervour died.
Harold had earned the vengeance sought
though stalled conquest much hurt had brought.

Thus now he yearned for well-earned peace 855
to mourn the dead and war to cease.
The benign King much mercy showed
in pardoning captives who owed
their lives to him for their vile crimes
upon England in cruel times. 860
Orkney's two earls he thus did give
their own freedom — their lives to live.
To return hence to their cold Isles
upon an oath as King's exiles.

The Nordic threat had been repelled 865
and war's embers were duly quelled.
Yet now remained that mournful task
to bury friends and their grace ask.
Among the dead, Leofwin stared
at that wrung face, lifeless and scared. 870
Young Leofstan, bound to this quest,
lay on the ground in lasting rest.
Bitter bewailed the Saxon lord
his haughty words as battle soared.
His heart was struck by guilt foisted 875
as Saxon flags were now hoisted.

Evening settled. Voices were low.
The battlefield in lights did glow.
Prayers were told and dirges sung
while much anguish their drained hearts stung. 880

The Hæstingas, what few remained,
carried aloft with souls much pained,
Gyrth's royal bier. That burden light
they bade farewell in endless night.
"The old linger, the young perish.   885
No more shall they their lives cherish.
Alas! To bear God's secret ways,
and live out long these wicked days."
The King thus spoke by barrow sealed.
Close to the sea his grief soon healed.   890
For Leofwin tears fell down hard.
By woe engulfed his soul was marred.

As those brothers in silence mourned
there soon came word of warning scorned.
A lone rider rode through the dark.   895
Bishop Stigand bid King to hark:
"Lord! Woe besets once more thy shores.
Thou seem fated to fight more wars.
For there now looms a threat long feared.
The Norman Duke more blood has smeared.   900
Bid men march swift towards the south
and force thy foes into a rout.
On English soil much blood was shed.
Hastings was felled and folk lie dead."

Those words of doom Leofwin heard,   905
while Elvyn's face through darkness stirred.

CANTO II

The sound of waves swept overhead
as he stumbled as one thus dead.

Interlude I

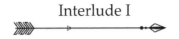

Behold! That warrior weary was
gazing ahead with such lost cause.
Sitting as one slumped dead by grief;
bereft of love, life lived so brief.
The wind yet hissed through swaying trees   5
and with it brought a restful breeze.
Through scattered clouds the peering sun
in warm embrace joyous light spun.
At that lone lord the old man smiled
with gentle face that Time defied.   10
The host dared ask once more earnest
what came to pass to his frail guest.

After a while Leofwin sighed
and with a gleam that old man eyed.
He slowly stood, armour clinking,   15
and limped forward silent, thinking.
His body bent with weariness
ached bitterly in his distress.
In that cool breeze he thus shuddered,
till suddenly few words uttered: 20
"Of God's most grand designs on earth
to fairest beauty He gave birth.
Thus wounding soul with so much pain
once Elvyn's love I sought to gain.

An angel bright and hope to Man   25
was ever the Creator's plan.
A Queen amid Nature's splendour
and majesty, yet so tender.
Alas! Her grace my soul did clasp
beyond the reach of mortal grasp.   30
And she for whom I long to seek
once more I wish to hear her speak.
Her face akin the light of day,
my heart delights in childish play.
Her voice as soft as a caress   35
brings peace to mind and soul does bless.
My undimmed praises hereby end
for no more hope is there to spend.
Yet love for her remains as clear.
Everlasting, I hold it dear. "   40
That warrior sad slunk back weary
down on the bench and most dreary.
No more he spoke. Low hung his head.
Stricken by grief his heart then bled.
The night arrived at sun's descent   45
behind the hills as light was spent.
There sat those men in silence deep
where thoughts break free and shadows creep.
That place so fair grew cold as death.
Naught else called out but the wind's breath.   50

Canto III

Shadows were long, the sun was set.
A hapless cry the forest beset.
Through fen and plain and every brook
a crashing noise the earth thus shook —
as if the wind with violence   5
tore down those trees by God's vengeance.
A sword was swung, ruthless it clove,
and down tumbled an entire grove.
Upon rumours that Normans purged
the southern shores and conquest urged,   10
as England reeled and neared its end,
Harold once more sought to defend.
When that foreboding news they heard
the wills of all were greatly stirred.
But none more so was Leofwin   15
so torn by grief and rage within.
An unmatched feat more worth of song
as journey swift though miles were long,
thus Harold's men marched south in haste.
Normans to face and lives to waste.   20
Though much wearied by heavy toil,
in stubborn mind their hearts did boil.
Their homeland throbbed by new danger
as Duke William planned to conquer.

Towards the southeast coast there lay 25
a vast woodland dreary and grey.
That wooded mass for miles it spread
and its long path to Hastings led.
Harold's army had reached the field
before the trees of that dark Weald[1]. 30
Beyond that woodland, vast and dense,
there lay Hastings's broken defence.
As they approached the forest dark
behind it rose a vision stark.
Under the cloudy sky of night 35
a fiery glow shone fierce and bright.
Yet shadows deep lay before those
who came in haste to face their foes.
Those men then knew their homes were lost,
while cruel thoughts stabbed like deep frost. 40

Among them was Leofwin grim
who now in rage again swung firm.
Once more amid the crippled trees,
with flaming blade he felled with ease.
Words reached his ears from solemn mouth 45
that Elvyn fair had fled the south.
To keep folk safe, towards the North,
with many kin she journeyed forth.
From Norman threat she hoped to flee
and seek refuge far from the sea. 50
Yet rumours spread that she was caught

within that Weald with snares so fraught.
Leofwin roared in grief unquenched.
His worn armour in sweat was drenched.
That man soon fell on ground kneeling.   55
His breaths heavy — on sword reeling.

With wary step the King drew near
to Leofwin, to brother dear:
"My mind is set, I will not yield
to thy counsel to pass through Weald."   60
Thus spoke Harold in quiet voice
as he renounced his brother's choice.
"Although our quest yonder now lies,
I will not risk men's swift demise.
My heart burns hot in need to fight   65
against this long-expected plight.
Yet wisdom warns me not to march
through that accurséd forest's arch.
It pains me much and strikes me cold
to see how all these woes unfold.   70
By longer ways will I confront
those foes who now our folk do hunt,
and thus shall I avoid this Weald
and all its malice now concealed.
I give to thee consent to seek   75
such hopeless paths whose ends are bleak.
Yet Love beyond a King's own need
do I see clear and plainly read.

I pray to God your soul to guard
ere near the end your wit discard." 80

Then silent stood Leofwin bent.
His sword in hand, his anger spent.
A hush then fell and men shuddered.
The King's brother these words uttered:
"Harold my kin, attend to me! 85
England I hold as dear as thee.
Yet as thou claim, my love for her
the stronger burns and heart does stir.
I therefore seek a swifter way
back to Elvyn through forest fey. 90
Such evil that my road might haunt
mars[2] not my will nor heart does daunt.
The swiftest way to reach our foes
is through that path beset by woes.
'Tis not my wish to challenge thee 95
who on good will now sets me free.
I understand thy need to take
other roads long ere foes thou break.
You need more men to help thus fight
those Norman dogs who now cause plight. 100
Towards the east it would be wise,
and thus come south where threat now lies,
to march thy host swift as may be
and rally men to fight for thee.
Yet I shall choose my own sure fate 105

as need drives me thus borne by hate.
Ere Weald defeats me and death calls,
I pray no doom upon thee falls."

And thus it was as dawn dispelled
the night shadows and fears were quelled,   110
Leofwin chose companions true.
What perils lay none there then knew.
To aid their lord they now gathered
six in all in raiment tattered.
Beornræd and Algar brave —   115
those Hæstingas glory did crave.
The warmonger, fierce Eoforhild,
with brother marched, Elric keen-skilled.
Those axe-wielders one there then knew
as kinswoman their ranks joined too.   120
Thus Ashlea from King's household,
with strength of mind and heart so bold,
declared to them her wish to serve
the King's brother and oath observe.
"I will not be forsaken so   125
to fend our home and anguish sow,
while my brothers for England fight
and those heathens ravage and smite."
Fair words she spoke ere host had sped
unto Jórvik where blood was shed.   130
In that onset her grit revealed,
against Norsemen with sword and shield.

These worthy souls Leofwin led
through forest arch where branches bled,
and crookéd roots the path waylaid   135
yet none of them their lord betrayed.
Nor did Hrodulf, relic-bearer,
who owed his life to God's saviour.
Grasping a sword the gloom he eyed
and would not part from his lord's side.   140
These names are famed in English lore
and Saxons brave to God thus swore:
"The King's brother we will not fail,
and thus in Faith we shall prevail."

The blazing glow by now had waned   145
yet clouds of smoke the sky now stained
and birds of prey with evil cries
circled above like devils' spies.
In saddle sat Harold silent
bidding farewell those souls intent,   150
as deep they plunged into the bleak
tangled forest beneath the reek.
The light of day was left behind
once deep they stepped in Weald unkind.
The stir outside of marching hosts   155
echoed akin to restless ghosts.
Struck by dew drops as cold as death
down from the trees like giants' breath,
the brave Saxons followed the way

where watchful roamed some unseen prey.   160
No leaves rustled, no branches stirred.
No birds did sing, no voices heard.
Some evil reigned which brought unease
as fog soon stalked the twisted trees.

The coarse harsh sound of roots decayed   165
by heavy tread were crushed and splayed.
The creaking shields and clinking mail
did harm the peace and silence frail.
The shadows preyed upon their sights;
their minds deceived by grotesque wights[3].   170
Within each tree there seemed to dwell
many doomed souls screaming from Hell.

Now far ahead Leofwin strode.
With sword in hand its edges glowed.
His eyes aware of shadows deep   175
which lay before him set to leap.
The others followed soon behind
yet seeping fog had made them blind.
Their lord they missed in murky veil
as whispers rose to a fierce wail.   180
Hrodulf cowered beside Elric.
Old fears assailed that young cleric.
In haste the fog they breached and nigh
they found their lord with sword held high.
He stood on guard, tense and steadfast,   185

while the others round him amassed,
forming a wall of shields all set
ready to smite the unseen threat.

The silent air was much oppressed
amid the breaths of those whose quest   190
led them so deep in that cursed Weald.
Though none of them to fear did yield.
"My friends, my kin, hold firm thy will.
Let no hearts sink to deadly chill."
Thus spoke their lord, whose sword blazed bright,   195
kindling the fog with fiery light.
Then suddenly a dark shadow
the murky veil pierced with a glow.
Two reddened eyes peered through the gloom,
fast approaching — proclaiming doom.   200
The fog succumbed to the black cloud
as the great beast, in shadowed shroud,
hindered the path and roared with rage
with hind legs bent set to engage.
The massive wolf with blazing gaze   205
and fiery mouth threatened their days.
As those brave souls their shields then raised.
In silence each the Lord they praised.
With shield still slung behind his back
and sword in hand, no strength did lack.   210
Forward he strode to face the beast
which now was reared ready to feast.

A deep growl fled from its vile maw
and its harsh mane at neck did claw.
The barghest's[4] teeth, with fierce fire licked,   215
keenly now sought death to inflict.
The beast was bred in that fell world
where devils dwell, and here was hurled
as Man's worst bane to haunt this wood
and bring much angst to all that's good.   220

Beornræd and Eoforhild,
stepping forward, by thirst were filled
to fight the beast and pierce its skin
to claim the praise of Leofwin.
Their sword and axe they firmly clenched   225
and swift strode forth with fears now quenched.
The barghest growled with eyes of lust
at mortal men whose strength did trust.
"Stand down my friends, for thy doom lies
beyond this Weald under dark skies.   230
By God proclaimed I forth now set
to smite this beast and quell its threat."
Those Saxons stood silent in awe
as their own lord his sword did draw.
Mighty Fyrecg was flaming fierce.   235
Leofwin leapt ready to pierce.
The barghest charged heedless of blade.
Its biting howl shuddered that glade,
splintered the trees and cracked the earth

as both engaged in clash of worth.   240

Never was such a tale of dread,
written on page nor justly said,
of how those two titans of war
were locked in clash of strength and gore.
Violent blows were struck in haste   245
and blood flowed swift by pride misplaced.
The wolf-phantom and Leofwin —
each lunged to pierce the other's skin.
The famed warriors did gaze in awe
as their captain escaped that maw.   250
Through molten flesh he thrust his sword
while each blow weakened that staunch lord.
Yet Ashlea and Eoforhild,
with all the rest their blood was thrilled.
Bidden to watch the heinous fight,   255
they were beset by unseen plight.

Vicious wild wolves through mirk appeared,
and rushed in haste with wrath all smeared.
Through thinning fog they now did swarm
around those souls like swirling storm.   260
With axes, swords and shields in hand
they held their ground to a firm stand.
And Hrodulf too, who fought for life,
clutched firm his shield and raised his knife.
With steady heart and face all grim,   265

withstood the fear which assailed him.
Meanwhile their lord still battled long
with the barghest whose might was strong.
The wolves that now ran through the glade,
unlike the beast whom lord now preyed,   270
came swiftly down in thirst and wrath:
with starving eyes and mouths all froth.
With a keen scent and lust for blood,
more than a score rushed like a flood,
barking and howling through the dell   275
and screaming cries straight out of hell.

Such prowess none shall ever see,
of swords thus wielded with great glee
as Hæstingas, of whom those two,
Beornræd and Algar slew.   280
Cleaving through fangs and shearing skins
as scythes through wheat they purged their sins.
Those two famed men kept wolves at bay
and swords reddened by fallen prey.
Neither has song ever been sung   285
of Elric's wrath in battle flung.
Equalled only by Eoforhild
who with sure strokes wolves swiftly killed.
Amid that clash of savagery,
when beast and man strove in fury,   290
there rose a voice above the cries,
soft yet steadfast which reached the skies.

Herein lies told of such spirit
as Ashlea's unquestioned grit.
Many fell wolves felt the keen bite 295
and bitter edge of her skilled fight.

While blows thundered and howls still roared,
there came upon the Saxon lord
the barghest's jaws with strength renewed
to quench his life and end the feud. 300
It clung madly to his right arm
with force to break and to disarm,
biting through flesh and sinew deep
as blood through hellish fangs did seep.
While life faltered from aching wound, 305
his sword turned dim by cold consumed.
From grasp it fell into the mud
to drown there deep in pools of blood.
The beast tightened its cruel grasp
as Leofwin for air did gasp. 310
He fell down swift upon the ground,
as torment deep his life had bound.
Glancing behind, his eyes beheld
those loyal friends who wolves still felled,
while corpses filled that evil glade 315
and presently assault was stayed.
Their rounded shields were much battered,
swords and axes notched and shattered.
Eyes grimed with sweat and their foes' gore,

yet in dim light stout stares still bore. 320

Then God's chosen rose to his feet.
In agony he felt the heat
that draped the beast while fires burst
and it glowered with ravenous thirst.
With his left hand he grasped its snout 325
and freed himself with raucous shout.
The deadly fangs flesh pierced no more
still blood gushed out — on path did pour.

Leofwin struck a potent fist
which broke its jaw, while mouth did twist. 330
The Saxon lord, not yet content,
clutched firm its neck and head he bent.
He crushed its skull with divine will
as from its jaws swift fled a shrill.
A roaring wail thus left the beast 335
as it fell down — from life released.
The few fell wolves howled their lament
and swiftly fled — their lust now spent.
Their cries soon failed, silence returned,
as God's warriors evil had spurned. 340
Thus stunned awhile by stirring sight,
of fallen foe by their lord's might,
the spent Saxons came to his aid
as Leofwin stumbled and swayed.
They huddled round him grimacing 345

at grisly gash, its blood sizzling.
Yet with stern face he looked ahead
along the road where his quest led.
"My lord, thy deeds this day shall be
forever praised. Eternally.   350
Yet even thou must rest awhile
from weary toil and dire trial."
Ashlea spoke, her voice gentle,
while Hrodulf cleansed the wound with skill.
The others looked upon dead foes   355
swallowed by fog which soon arose.
"Nay, it is ill to dwell much long
amid these trees where beasts belong.
The road lies long upon this quest,
ere we can earn our needed rest.   360
Yet even now, driven by need,
my heart is set to give such heed
and purge this Weald from all evil,
so God's great grace we shall instil."
Amid grim smile Leofwin spoke.   365
Although in pain, he looked in turn
at each of those before him stern.
Each one of them a loyal friend
who followed him to such dark end.
Amid the shrouds of rising fog   370
and dark shadows that sights did clog,
the Saxons marched with backs now bent,
their vigour dim and strength thus spent.

For miles they trudged well through the night.
Their heavy breaths the air did smite   375
as they stumbled and almost fell
on rough-hewn road leading to Hell.
Upon the ground without regard,
heedless to set a futile guard,
they cast themselves beside a tree —   380
devoid of strength and light to see.
In weariness they thus succumbed
seeking their rest as peril shunned.
No fires were lit nor songs were sung
as one by one to sleep all clung.   385

Deep in the night Leofwin saw
a vision clear of doubt and awe.
From darkness deep a light did loom —
casting shadows, dispelling gloom.
Though candle dim it held in sight,   390
the figure shone with inner light.
The phantom's tresses gently flew
in the stale air where no leaf blew.
That pale face glanced, sad and forlorn,
at Saxon lord whom grief had worn.   395
The slender stature of the bride,
with piercing eyes, humbled his pride.
Her light approached till Leofwin
his love kindled from deep within,
as he beheld his treasured wife   400

who seemed altered, bereft of life.
Desire took hold of him to stand
and take his wife by fragile hand —
embracing her, while cursing fate
that drove them thus away of late. 405
Yet limbs and heart felt cold as stone.
His voice failed him, as did each bone,
while the phantom sailed over him
bearing candle ever so dim.

With silence hushed and peace complete, 410
there rose whispers of voice so sweet
borne on a wind from distant shores
to mortal lands pure from all wars:
"Heed boding words, O Godwin's son!
England's freedom thou must not shun. 415
Thy brother's need is now more dire
than thine own quest that ends in fire.
Make haste and flee this dread forest
where evils lurk and souls infest.
Doom is at hand when blood is spilt 420
and England falls by thine own guilt."
The candle's flame gave no more light,
as phantom wavered out of sight
leaving behind a silky trail
that soon vanished in misty veil. 425

Swift he awoke, Leofwin fair —

bereft of love, gasping for air.
No trace remained of nightly guest
as light of morn the east now blessed.
A few faint rays the dark roof clove,   430
through leaves and twigs that bright star drove.
The faint glimmer of a grey world
fell on his eyes as sight unfurled.
Doubt struck his heart with unease heft
at phantom's words of love bereft.   435
In earnest haste his mind did urge
once more to brave the forest's scourge.
His heart was wrung by fearful thought
in what cruel fate his wife was caught.
His heart was hot by fervent pain   440
to seek Elvyn and hold again.
Ere sun rose high he woke the rest
and urged them on while light still blessed:
"Be swift my friends! The night forebode
some wickedness beyond this road."   445
Eoforhild groaned as he staggered,
his gruff voice boomed and ears hammered:
"Never such mare[5] has stalked my sleep ,
as did last night upon me creep.
Let us depart this wicked place,   450
praying to God to grant us grace."
He grabbed his axe and shield he slung,
and swift behind the rest he sprung.

As day wore on and sky grew dim
those companions, nimble and grim,   455
kept to the path oppressed by trees
and made their way with much unease.
Birds had returned and joyful sang,
in earnestness their voices rang.
A gentle breeze caressed the air,   460
bringing relief while woe did bear.

Swift now they marched through the Weald's gloom
eager to end that quest of doom,
and feel once more the deep sea's breath
from southern shores, away from death.   465
But Leofwin was deep in thought.
In silence walked while doubt he fought.
The wound still ached and phantom's haunt
troubled his mind — his heart did taunt.

The sun soon dipped towards the west   470
as Saxons craved once more some rest.
Beside a stone their arms they laid
which stood erect, by Time decayed.
Next to the path, like a bird's claw,
upon that stone those Saxons saw   475
such curious runes and dark markings —
of obscure signs and strange carvings.
While mortal lands in twilight basked,
night soon returned and forest masked.

The thick fog stalked their steps anew 480
as wicked howls echoed and flew.

"My sword now thirsts for blood unspilt
and would rejoice with hand on hilt,
than lie yearning in scabbard cold
taunted by cries none can behold," 485
thus Algar spoke in furtive tone.
While Eoforhild, by laughter prone,
his harsh mirth broke the rife stillness;
his booming voice raised to excess.
The Saxon lord reproached his friend, 490
sensing peril from some portend.
And while his voice yet still echoed,
a perverse laugh thus soon followed.
Those Saxons brave rose to their feet
at ghastly call though its tone sweet. 495
It smote the air, haunting their ears,
while its oddness kindled new fears.
A childish cackle mocked their wills,
piercing their hearts with deathly chills.
No sooner had its echo died 500
than a new laugh relief denied.
Those companions with shields held tight
and arms grasped firm ready to fight,
stood still — watchful — in gathered gloom
while the dense fog closer did loom. 505
Leofwin raised Fyrecg his sword

and, as the rest followed their lord,
plunged through dark — wary and strained.
While shields they raised, much scored and stained.
Another laugh they now did hear,   510
sometimes away, other times near.
A graceful voice, a melody.
A hideous cry, a mockery.

With night fallen, all light was choked.   515
What threat approached the dark now cloaked.
Their fire sputtered and warmth now sent,
filling the air with burning scent.
"Dear God our Lord, grant us thy light
to keep us safe and dispel night."   520
Hrodulf shuddered, shaking with dread.
He clutched his cross, praying instead.
"Hush!" cried Elric, wielding his axe,
"My blood is chilled by hellish cracks.
Hush! There it smites once more close by   525
that youthful laugh — its tone so wry."

On a sudden a blaze then shone
not far away from runic stone.
Over water, amid a glade,
flickered a light — gently it swayed.   530
Wisps of green flame quivered and spat
over a pond so dark, whereat
the crooked tree roots reaching down deep

their thirst they quenched — deeper did creep.
Leofwin strayed towards the light,   535
while the others beheld that sight.
In darkness plunged, the path they lost,
as mortal Time beyond it crossed.
"My friends and kin, we come at last
to the Weald's heart, where Satan cast   540
his vile delight — where demons crawl
to bring despair and woe to all.
My heart warns me that here dwells one
who long ago God's light did shun.
To the Lord's wrath dared not to yield   545
and now spreads ills throughout this Weald.
I bid thee come and follow me
to oust evil, by Christ's decree.
I falter not. My will is set
to face alone the Devil's threat."   550
Grinning he spoke. His breath quickened.
He walked towards the light strengthened.

Fyrecg's spirit through veins did flow,
whose divine grace in blade did show.
In wounded hand strong held his sword   555
and heedless trudged that fearless lord.
Though bloodied gash did pain him still,
vigour returned with hardened will.
Then Algar urged his lord to judge
if cause was right ere pride begrudge: 560

"I bid thee stay and pursue not
that wicked flame though blood flows hot.
We must return to path assigned
and find the way. For in my mind
I see the edge where trees do fail   565
and sun and stars forever sail.
We came to seek those who are lost,
who fled in fear from Norman host.
Not least thy wife, who rumours said
her urgent strides somewhere here led."   570
That Saxon man spoke wise and true.
Yet such true words he stern did rue.
Still Leofwin, on light now bent,
grinned at his friend ere onwards went.
Daring and strong he wavered not   575
but steadfast led, while fear forgot —
as one thus seized by such sheer zeal
seeks to discern what could reveal.

His companions followed behind.
Less willingly were they inclined   580
to seek the cause of flaming sight.
Yet true to word they chose aright.
The light floated in verdant green
above the lake's darkening sheen.
Leofwin, awed by flame so pure,   585
was strongly bound by its allure.
Sword he lowered, to knees he fell.

The keen light danced causing a swell.
Ripples rang out along the lake
licking tree roots by water's wake.   590
The others too, who joined their lord,
gripped by stupor, dropped axe and sword
as they beheld the flame's own charm
which seemed so fair and caused no harm.
The light strengthened and swelled in size,   595
burning radiant, blinding their eyes.
On a sudden a voice arose
so soft and sweet that senses froze.
A song unfurled which filled the glade,
its chants so pure that movements swayed.   600
The Saxons stood with mouths agape
while flame transformed into a shape.
A graceful voice then sang to tune
with words so fair that hearts were hewn.
Leofwin too was swiftly stunned   605
as urgent quest he now had shunned.
Fyrecg slipped from his crippled hand.
Shields were lowered, on ground did land.
Men's limbs faltered, no strength they bore,
while that song's might surged all the more.   610
Ashlea too, with mind discreet
ever wary, perceived deceit.
Yet her senses were overcome
and soon fell down by lake all numb.
The shape amid the dancing flame   615

appeared before those warriors tame.
It stepped out from the dazzling flare.
Across the lake strode through the air.

As blinded eyes submitted to
the burning light which stronger grew,   620
a woman's limbs and flowing hair
they saw take form — splendid and fair.
Yet even though the flame thus splayed,
a growing dark enclosed that glade.
Impervious, a cloud of night   625
circled warriors — strangling all light.
The cleric Hrodulf — weak of mind —
that man of God, though awed and blind,
his heart consumed by doubt and care
uttered in thought the Lord's prayer.   630
The others still did gaze unto
that shape silent who gently drew
towards those men and woman still,
as stifling air turned to a chill.
The cross's sign Hrodulf then made,   635
and God's mercy in earnest bade.

Thereupon the voices floundered.
The music ceased and song faltered.
While thunder groaned and light tarnished,
the earth then shook — vision vanished.   640
Those Saxons caught still by the spell

crept near a tree and weary fell.
Though song had ceased and darkness came,
that fay[6] shone bright with inner flame.
Clad in long robes of silky green   645
forth nimbly came that woodland queen.

Canto IV

Leofwin gained his ground in plight,
while to him sped a bright green light.
From that woman, splendid and fair,
a voice emerged concealed with care:
"O Leofwin, whose deeds are famed   5
throughout England, where foes lie tamed;
O fateful friends who claim such quests
now rest awhile and be my guests.
I welcome you to my own home
where thy desires are free to roam.   10
Come! do not fear the nightly cries,
but set at peace thy weary eyes.
Come closer now and do not stray.
Such needless toil now wash away.
Leave crookéd path and with me dwell,   15
and bid troubles a fond farewell."
With arms outstretched, that smiling fay
greeted Saxons at end of day.
Her robes fluttered in curious guile,
for no breeze blew nor airs did pile.   20

As gloom succumbed to fay's caress,
a light appeared which did impress
a faint likeness of lone dwelling

amid the trees where life did cling.
Beside the lake, now cold and clear,   25
the thatched structure through gloom did peer.
With walls concealed where ivy crept,
the leaves were lush with vines well kept.
A stony path from lake there strayed
upon which weary feet were laid.   30
A low arched door stood at its end
where shadows lurked and light did blend.
A candle bright, through window stained,
its keen flame kissed the sill all veined.
While woodland sprite the door unlocked,   35
the others soon behind her walked.

Leofwin's mind, not yet all dumb,
nor drunken by promised welcome,
struggled to speak before that queen
and used his sword as staff to lean: 40
"O fairest fay of woodland glade,
why do thou seek to give us aid?
'Tis not our aim from path to stray
so close by edge where lies the way.
Through Weald our path has led in haste.   45
Though still we knew, evil we faced;
that wickedness which lies in wait,
ready to pounce on prey in hate.
A tough and weary road we met,
beset by woes, ensnared in net   50

woven by fate which mocks our pride
and yet wolves' fangs we still defied.
Be not silent and truth now tell
of why thy voice rings like a spell.
Ere one more step to thee consent   55
I must now know thy true intent."
Though strong in word, his heart faltered
at woman's smile. His stance shattered.
Closer he strode towards the door
while stepping back to days of yore.   60
That woodland fay held out her hand,
on the doorstep in timeless land.

There softly swelled her soothing voice
as she proclaimed Leofwin's choice:
"For far beyond this woodland fair   65
I hear whispers where tales declare
that King Harold plans worthy schemes
while England's fate waivers in dreams.
Come closer now ere news grows old
and take refuge from rampant cold.   70
Come closer now and seek thy rest
and lay aside such futile quest."
Leofwin, dazed and overcome
by fair woman, there did succumb.
Holding her hand he passed within.   75
followed swiftly by Saxon kin.
And thus it was after long days

of trials and angst in wooded maze,
those travellers earned needed rest
in timeless glade where darkness pressed.   80
Yet all the while they there abode,
the light of day did seem bestowed
upon Saxons. No light it was
from sun or star, nor obvious cause.
Its radiant beams on house alone   85
and silent lake were keenly thrown.
That nightly glade, at first thought grey,
now basked in never-ending day.

The quest aside they freely laid.
Their minds flooded by visions weighed,   90
gifted with life which did but please;
bereft of all mortal unease.
Thus unaware of a real world
beyond the woods where Time unfurled,
their hearts were bound to that lone den   95
in that Weald's heart — the plague of men.
"O fair lady, what is thy name?
For I would sing thy praise in fame
and thus declare to all mankind
what tame being lies here confined."   100
Leofwin spoke in mind's delight
while woman stood before his sight.
She smiled with eyes that could enchant
and her response willing did grant:

"My name is now long lost from lore   105
amid that past which lives no more.
Yet once a time folk used to say:
'There goes Glaistig that timid fay!'"

***

As days went by, Leofwin kept
his sword in scabbard safely wrapped;   110
ever present beside him lay,
during his rest or waking day.
Ever eager the fay thus bade
to look upon that renowned blade.
Anxious she urged the Saxon lord,   115
yet he denied the grasp of sword.
She pleaded long with Leofwin
yet never scorn she showed therein,
and in kindness her guests treated
while their requests keenly greeted.   120

Algar and Eoforhild, meanwhile,
forgot their woes and weary trial.
Beornræd and Elric too,
their doubts and fears they swiftly slew.
Thus far away their troubles fled   125
and so did any thoughts of dread.
They drank and sang and wandered free
beside the lake — ever in glee.

Within its waters, that fay kind,
their armour laved[1] and grace assigned.   130
Her tresses long and robes she bore
lay scattered on the lake's damp shore.
There she would sing with voice dazzling
while water poured on their clothing,
washing away the battle stains   135
as Saxons gazed, relieved from pains.

Ringing ripples of waters cool
danced before them around the pool.
Their shields and swords in slumber eased
while music swelled and their ears pleased.   140
Where once they thought that glade perverse,
and to dark lake they were averse,
ere flame appeared on that first night,
they never saw such wondrous sight.
And Hrodulf too, that man of God,   145
succumbed to bliss as his heart thawed.
His mind subdued by queen of worth,
forsook the Cross and joined in mirth.

Amid their joys, there grew mistrust —
much doubts and fears at what was just   150
plagued Ashlea's own muddled mind
to which the others seemed so blind.
Her heart misgave her when she saw
their quest ignored while Time did gnaw.

The Saxon lord she sought to urge   155
of days wasted by woodland's scourge.
Yet Leofwin, oblivious was
to her pleading at needless cause.
He thus did speak to ease her dread
and fear dismiss while concern shed: 160
"O brave woman and loyal friend
thy true concern I do commend.
No cause have thou to doubt our host,
where our wounds heal and triumphs boast.
We thus shall not our stay prolong,   165
till our minds rest and limbs grow strong
for what must come beyond this Weald
where doom awaits and fates lie sealed."

As sun fell down o'er mortal world,
a nightly shade through glade unfurled.   170
Those warriors spent with feast and drink,
lay down to rest beside lake's brink.
Leofwin lay soon serf to sleep.
His mind wandered while dreaming deep,
in paths unknown and thoughts revealed,   175
perceiving much secrets concealed.
Amid the visions stark and clear,   .
a light there shone soothing and dear.
By its radiance all dreams faltered.
As it approached his thought altered.   180
Once more there stood the fragile face

of phantom kind, undimmed by grace.
Though candle held, no flame burnt fierce,
yet inner light through breast did pierce.
Leofwin's bride with sad eyes gazed   185
at her husband, who looked on dazed.
Her voice then rose once more to tell
and warn of that which soon befell:
"Heed well my words, O Leofwin!
Tarry not far from thine own kin.   190
England lies poised on edge of doom
while thou lie snared in wretched gloom.
Awake! and flee from this dwelling.
Find thy way back to the living.
Awake! Make haste ere Harold falls   195
and linger not in devil's thralls!"

With phantom gone and vision lost,
Leofwin woke to morning frost.
He lay on moss, rough and sodden,
amid sharp rocks deeply trodden.   200
Standing slowly against a tree,
while others slept in tranquil glee,
he saw Glaistig approach discreet
ever silent, with supple feet.
The Saxon lord by smile disarmed.   205
That woman's glance his mind had charmed.
She thus gestured at bench by lake
and sat down too, ere rest did wake.

Her humble voice quivered in fret.
Her eyes both shy, her cheeks scarlet.   210
She smiled again clenching his heart —
that piercing gaze, an arrow's dart.
"With open arms I welcomed thee,
and glad am I of company.
Thy mirth and glory fills this Weald,   215
its wickedness and darkness healed.
A few more days I bid you stay
for 'tis not late to find your way.
So rest a while, thy health restore
away from pain and far from war."   220
Her eyes on his she closer leaned.
Piercing pupils green-hued thus beamed.

They struck his heart with sheer delight.
Her charming voice, mind did excite.
Yet while he lay in dreamlike daze,   225
heedless to him, at sword did gaze
that woodland fay. While voice still spilt,
her hand reached out at pommel gilt.
Her eyes widened with blatant lust
and in her strength did blindly trust.   230
In arrogance of her own thought
Glaistig faltered — pride overwrought.
Ere tender fingers touched the blade
a cloud of gloom conquered the glade.
Thunder rumbled and the ground cracked,   235

a howling roar the silence wrecked.
A strong gust stirred of wind rushing,
tugging at trees and grass crushing.
Fierce boiled the lake, bubbling in ire,
now turned so dark and wild with fire. 240
Though morn was young, the light then failed.
Darkness smothered all life now veiled.
That fair dwelling whence rest was gained
fell in decay while lush was stained.
The veined ivy shrivelled to rot. 245
Its ashen vines soon blew to naught.
With faces gnarled and vicious grins,
the crippled trees shed their smooth skins.

Those Saxons woke to throbbing world,
their rest disturbed by wrath unfurled. 250
Amid clamour, their shields they missed,
axes and swords misplaced from fist.
Meanwhile their lord, from stupor free,
unleashed his sword, eager to flee;
while fay in anguish wailed much pained. 255
Touching the blade, her hand now stained.
Her screech shrivelled the earth around.
Thus was the peaceful silence drowned.
While Fyrecg shone, her arm inflamed.
The fay's lament their senses maimed. 260
From lake there burst spirits wailing —
robed all in white, lank hair trailing.

Their shrills shrieking, unbearable.

Their pallid faces, terrible.

Mouths open wide and eyes of death   265

chilled heart and bones with frozen breath.

A score or more from waters rose,

while Saxons' limbs by screams thus froze.

Those spectres clutched with claws like knives,

while mortal souls fought for their lives.   270

Dazed and disturbed, flung into fray,

they strove to keep their foes at bay.

Four Shadows flew at Eoforhild.

Their hellish cries his heart had chilled.

Onto that warrior swift they clung   275

driving their claws as flesh they stung.

That man roared loud, his strength futile.

As those Shadows, vicious and vile,

dragged him far down into the lake

causing a swirl through giant wake.   280

As deep they plunged, a scarlet trail

stained the surface of waters frail.

Thus passed in haste brave Eoforhild;

of warriors strong not the least skilled.

Grieving in mind at fallen friend,   285

those Saxons faced such brutal end.

Forced to succumb to Shadows' might —

their limbs helpless, bereft of fight.

Yet Leofwin, engulfed by woe,

summoned his strength upon that foe.   290

He unleashed rage on laughing fay
who mocked in mirth at stricken prey.
Elric and Algar, with clenched fists,
thrust off spectres while dragged from wrists
towards the lake, churning in ire,   295
to the same fate in blooded mire.
Beornræd, with savage force,
thrust off a Shadow, shrieking coarse.
Ere he had time to set off free,
four more pinned him against a tree.   300
Ashlea too, whose shield had found,
withheld their blows down on the ground.

Hrodulf in fear, God did exalt,
while no Shadow dared him assault.
While attack surged, that woodland hag,   305
revealed to them her true form's rag.
Fair skin decayed, by Time battered;
her splendid robes, soaked and tattered.
Upon her face a hideous change.
Leofwin's gaze fell on sight strange.   310
No graceful glance nor lustful eyes.
That grinning witch held no more guise.
Though stunned by ruse, the Saxon lord
held to his wits and grasped his sword.
With mighty cry he lunged onto   315
the wicked hag — her head to hew.
Ere neck he reached and sword he swung,

Shadows screaming to him thus clung
and threw him down with limbs so thin,
whilst sharpened claws pierced through his skin.   320
Though overwhelmed, his will hardened.
God's voice he heard borne on the wind.
He freed himself from stringent hold.
With flaming sword Shadows did scold.

In bloodied glade noise did arise,   325
of haunted shrills and mortal cries.
Dark was dispelled by wights[2] alight.
Saxons stood fast in furious fight.
Once more he strove, Leofwin brave,
to strike Glaistig and friends to save.   330
Yet once again his charge was foiled
by Shadows fell[3] who round him coiled.
His strength thus waned and blade he missed.
Fyrecg slipped down, as mud it kissed.
Still Shadows hissed in fear of sword;   335
hallowed by God — England to ward[4].

Glaistig advanced with evil lust.
From tattered robes a spear she thrust.
Dark words she spoke. With both hands laid,
she plunged it deep into the blade.   340
No tale tells how that spear was forged
nor on whose blood countless lives gorged.
Obsidian[5] head, iron-wrought shaft

spoke of prowess by hellish craft.
Evil spells coursed through Spear of War,   345
as dark glass pierced Fyrecg's deep core.
Such force was dealt that the ground burst
hurling all souls as light dispersed.
Fragments flew far from Fyrecg's blade.
A thousand flares scattered through glade.   350
While radiance hung o'er Saxons stunned,
the Shadows cowed and the light shunned.

Glaistig returned with wailing roar.
The spear in hand she lunged once more
to drive its head through Saxon's chest   355
and from his breast his soul thus wrest.
Leofwin felt his death swift neared.
That Spear of War he rightly feared.
To Elvyn fair his thought then fled,
for his lost wife his heart there bled.   360
In deep anguish wise words he heard
of that old man whose gift conferred.
Swift he unslung that wooden shield
which long he had refused to wield.
That fierce fay flew towards him raged   365
as ceaseless hate against him waged.
Leofwin raised the shield crusted.
In its woodcraft his life trusted.
Glaistig brought down the pointed shard.
The spear impaled that slender guard.   370

A shattered noise rose shrill and clear
as fragments flew from fractured spear.
The kneeling lord still held his shield —
no death plagued him nor did life yield,
as wicked fay was hurled away   375
by vicious blow aimed at her prey.

The blast echoed through darkened glade.
Stunned Leofwin weary then swayed.
While Glaistig groaned upon the grass,
a light appeared of shining glass.   380
Fyrecg's fragments rose through the air,
till swift they joined in blinding flare
to form a flame of light divine
that spilled forth bright and glade did shine.
A second sun seemed to ascend.   385
High up the trees the flame did wend.
No more darkness could eyes thus blind,
as comfort brought each mortal mind.
A golden light gleamed off the lake
as that Flame rose like coiling snake.   390
By tongues of fire tree trunks were licked
while the bright blaze keen cracked and clicked.
Seizing his chance, Leofwin rose
then fell back down as limbs thus froze;
his wounded arm subdued by pain   395
while weakness surged in every vein.
Her wits regained, Glaistig strode back

and with Shadows returned attack.
With Saxons freed and lord at hand,
to him they ran to put fierce stand.   400
Yet as Shadows, once more screaming,
scuttled back swift to lunge wailing,
their charge faltered by throbbing light,
and fled shrieking down lake in flight.

As silence set once more in haste,   405
Glaistig howling, agile thus paced.
Her will held fast, lusting to end
those mortal lives and their souls rend.
As she lunged forth and onwards came,
a shape stepped out from roaring Flame.   410
With hand outstretched towards the fay
she swift succumbed to flaming ray.
From tortured thing a shrill wail fled
as the keen Flame on hag thus fed.

Her brittle skin soon flaked to dust   415
as cloud of ash flew in a gust.
The shrieking cry trailed off now frail,
and thus the world no more would ail.
Silence once more reigned over Weald
and peace settled now woods were healed.   420
Leofwin strove with pain in hand,
while companions helped him to stand.
The figure bright spoke words to them.

From mouth unseen they clear did stem:
"Hail worthy Saxons brave and true!   425
Great deeds attained be not a few.
England's people will praise each name
unto Heaven, to high acclaim.
Yet pride for war and glory-keen,
while need to purge Weald's sins all clean,   430
shall cost you dear once woods you leave
and choices made, bitterly grieve.
Leofwin stay! Now hear me more:
thy doom awaits yonder in war;
away from Weald, under the sky,   435
on fateful field of battle nigh.
William the Duke assails the land.
Harold readies for hasty stand.
Though England scarred it still stands tall,
yet tide now turns to sure downfall.   440
Beware rumours that now far spread,
of fearsome knight whose mail shines red[6].
As yet unmatched his skill in war.
Dark spells he weaves, mighty in lore.
A loyal serf to Norman court,   445
wielding powers for kingly sport.
The Duke's army he now leads north
to face Harold who has set forth.
Though hallowed sword lies now shattered,
and thine own strength gravely battered,   450
the grace of God is with you all

until the end, till thy lives fall.
Now go in haste on path assigned
to reach Weald's edge and hope thus find.
Thy road is short ere thou news gain   455
where judgment waits among the slain."

That spirit bright then looked in turn
at each Saxon in gaze thus stern:
"No kindly words I offer thee
for dark the road lies by decree.   460
Beware thy strength O Algar true.
The Norman Duke's cousin now few
will challenge him to battle vain,
for by his sword many lie slain.
Meanwhile Elric, be not too rash   465
to seek thy foes in deadly clash.
Beornræd be not too bold
to bring down flag from bearer's hold.
Hrodulf thy faith, as man of God,
will prove stronger than bishop's laud.   470
Ashlea strong, in haste thou will
confront minstrel who sings with skill."
Its voice so pure as the sea's breeze,
wrought riddles dark and mind's unease.
While face nor form could they discern,   475
from that bright Flame no more did learn.
Kneeling in awe at divine light,
Leofwin bowed, though pain did smite.

In gratitude he praised God's grace
for aiding them in that vile place.   480

"Noble spirit in whose splendour
the world now basks in light tender.
We give thee thanks for thy warning.
Pray tell us now thy name to sing."
Leofwin spoke, dazzled by Flame,   485
while that figure pondered his claim.
Then angel bright, for so it was
as sent by God for divine cause,
did halt its speech and its grave word
the Saxon lord in grief now heard: 490
"O Leofwin, whose deeds shall be
forever known among folk free,
thy quest endeth for Elvyn wise,
for in this Weald were heard her cries.
Ere thou set forth with Harold King,   495
after the death of the Norse king,
thy fair wife fled from Norman force —
from southern coasts she forged her course.
Within this wood thy kin she led
to save their lives from the Duke's dread.   500
Forever praised her deeds now be,
for such stout heart is rare to see.
Yet veiled deceits were spun so deep,
within the Weald's dense trees did creep.
Till by the fay's foul guile were snared   505

those who in fear these woods had dared.
No soul now lives to tell the tale
of what befell by waters pale.
No hope remains, Elvyn to seek —
ere unseen fate beyond world bleak."   510

Leofwin fell stricken by woe
as ill words struck a deadly blow.
With mind engulfed by black despair
his thoughts drowned swift in that nightmare.
Long lay he there, still falling deep   515
in the abyss — in despair's keep.
Kneeling beside the somber lake
no wish he had ever to wake.
He rued the day he left her side
to seek glory in his false pride,   520
and fight a war that led to strife
so far away from his fair wife.
Countless the deaths he caused in vain
as King Harold, with many a thegn,
he urged in haste the North to wrest   525
from the Norse king at his behest.
In deep torment he now saw clear
what futile deeds and foolish fear
these wars breed for vainglory lords,
who seek only to drench their swords.   530
Yet as his mind saw a faint light
of life beyond that endless night,

the angel's words once more he heard,
of England's doom which close now neared.
But loath he was to be sundered   535
from Elvyn's love, and long wondered
how he dared hope to leave that Weald,
where his doomed fate was surely sealed.
In grim silence he vowed no more
to bear arms forth to any war.   540
Yet need then pressed him to make haste
to seek Harold — for battle braced.
His heart was wrung, though in his mind
a sliver thought, with hope defined,
keenly pierced through his black despair   545
as reason swelled — untarnished, fair.
The angel watched that lord's sorrow
in that undimmed heavenly glow.
Once Leofwin's resolve was clear,
that hallowed Flame spoke with words dear: 550
"Thy choice is made for one last task.
As for my name, for whom thou ask,
call me Micel[7] — remember plain,
for both our paths shall cross again."

Those grim Saxons bid it farewell,   555
as Flame rose high while light did swell.
From mortal world it passed away,
while the sun basked in a new day.
Evil shadows were now banished.

No hag there reigned — from earth vanished.　　560
The wholesome air blew fresh and keen
o'er ruined house by deep lake's sheen.
The signs of war that scarred the land
reminded them of fallen friend.
In sorrow sung a sour lament　　565
for Eoforhild, ere onwards went.
For Elyvn too and Saxon kin
a bitter dirge sang Leofwin.
Though Death triumphed Time still flew by,
while England's doom stalked ever nigh.　　570

Weapons and shields they found bestowed
in cold coffers from wrecked abode —
hammers and axes, swords and spears
from fallen men throughout the years.
Among the trove, Leofwin chose　　575
a slender axe to suit his throes.
The others too aged arms they took.
The Weald's perils they swift forsook.
The old man's shield, its worth upheld,
upon his arm he now firm held.　　580
His final fight would see him wield
that guard unto the battlefield.

Interlude II

Alas! The cry of Man's torment,
ere soul readies for Hell's descent.
Within those fields silence did loom,
yet voice rose high cursing its doom.
The soaked grass sighed, swaying and low.   5
Trees wailed wildly with wrathful woe.
Shy leaves shuddered in harsh sadness.
Mountains moaned in mourning madness.

Leofwin's rage roared on unquenched —
his heart and mind in fury drenched.   10
He wailed and howled, his anguish spilled,
while the old man with pity filled.
The King's brother, consumed by pain,
his wife had lost and angst did gain.
Solace he missed, his hope wore thin,   15
and no delight he found therein.

In pride and faith his home he left.
From Norse king's grasp quelled England's theft.
Through Weald he passed hoping to purge
such wickedness from woodland's scourge.   20
Bitter rueing his choice to leave
beloved home, his fate did weave.

In search of glory and deeds now vain,
no quest fulfilled nor hope did gain.

Down he fell, his strength now spent   25
and ire exhaled. By lake now bent,
he cursed himself at ill wisdom
and others' trust to follow him.
"Poor Eoforhild! Such Saxon true.
A mighty man whom Death thus slew.   30
Yet feast and mirth he will relish.
Heaven's glory shall embellish.
In God's own sight eternal lies,
as light undimmed graces his eyes."

Leofwin spoke with heart all wrung,   35
and mind much dazed where gloom now clung.
Upon the grass he sat all grey
as the old man beside him lay.
"Come! and dismiss thy needless cry.
None of thy deeds have gone awry.   40
Your love for kin and country fair
is but such life that mortals share.
Scold not thyself for choices made
through tangled fate before thee laid
ere thy own birth and rise to fame —   45
a humble pawn in life's great game.
Seek comfort friend! For no judgment
shall I declare on deeds well meant.

Thy tale soon ends. Be swift now tell
the truth of what gravely befell."   50

Canto V

Upon a time when eve returned,
and a cold wind the warm air spurned,
they reached the eaves of the forest
while brisk before them winter pressed.
Beornræd at moon did gaze,   5
grunting in thought at loss of days:
"My sight does seem to be awry
for a full moon graces the sky.
Yet but ten days 'tis since we walked
within the Weald and by ills stalked."   10
Leofwin too felt Time had played
some wicked trick and quest delayed.
"Nay my old friend. Thy sight lies not.
As Herald spoke, our path was fraught
with perils which have cost us days   15
from mortal world trapped in that maze."

Upon the plains and wind-swept fields
they marched silent with unslung shields.
Yet soon nearby, to Caldbec Hill[1],
the land did seem aflame by ill.   20
Thick fog enclosed that region's town,
while bright blazes buildings did drown.

As flames engulfed Leofwin's land,
the long-claimed doom was now at hand.

Ere noon had passed the sky grew dark.   25
An ill wind blew black clouds so stark.
From southern shore rushed scorching air,
as raging fires the land laid bare.
The deadly fumes the sun thus choked
and by such reek all light was cloaked.   30
The earth did groan, the world rumbled.
Southern England, by spell crumbled.
While Saxons brave in haste left Weald,
much ravaged fields their sights revealed.
Rivers glowed red, tree barks withered,   35
as Leofwin through charred grass slithered.
To his hometown, to Caldbec Hill,
they rushed in grief to wailings shrill.
A ruined mass of timber lay
consumed by blaze — at souls did flay.   40

Sharp screams rose high from searing dread
as doomed townsfolk in anguish fled.
Their cries soon died while flaming roars
rang in the air like songs of Wars.
Such wanton death and wicked deed,   45
in Saxon hearts despair did bleed.
Those companions their arms cast down
as they beheld that blazing town.

With heads bent low, in fires' light,
their souls cried out at bitter sight.   50
With spirits spent and strength shattered,
their last hope fled and swift scattered.

Though morn was young and fires now quenched,
a blackened gloom England still clenched.
Dark sorcery had rained on land   55
while woven spells the earth did brand.
As Hrodulf knelt and to God prayed,
to grant mercy on souls thus strayed,
Ashlea sang a dirge in praise
for fallen kin by cruel ways.   60
Above all pain her voice rose high,
and through the air traversed grim cry.
Though words were sad and mournful sung,
new hope kindled in hearts all wrung.
And Elric too in grief lay down   65
upon scorched ground near ashen town.
Beornræd, by Algar's side,
his shield unslung and sword swung wide.
Both Hæstingas, grim and silent,
upon ruins their gaze now bent.   70
Their grief equalled Leofwin's pain,
for their own kin were also slain.
Each Saxon gazed at town now lost,
while pondering how Weald had cost
such precious Time to reach the end   75

of their journey and woes amend.
On a sudden they all descried,
once dampened eyes had long since dried,
a sight so strange amid the heap
of ash and smoke where shade lay deep.   80
Elric in awe rose to his feet
and ventured forth, a child to greet.

A young man stood, stumbling forth lame,
ragged and scorched by deadly flame.
Eoforhild's kin rushed to his aid.   85
As the child came weary he swayed.
In Saxon's arms his frail head fell,
now swift released from Norman spell.
The others came and looked in dread
at hurt manling who from chest bled.   90
From that charred face keen eyes looked deep
ere child's weak voice from mouth did leap:
" 'Twas deadly rain of fire and ash
that smote the Hill and town did lash.
The belching smoke stained the black sky   95
and drowned the airs as lives did die.
The townsfolk screamed, shouting the name,
of ruthless man who land dared maim:
'The Red Knight comes! The Norman mage!
The Duke's army he leads in rage.'   100
So did they wail while their skins burned
and thus we knew the tide had turned.

Our King is lost, his men are ghosts,
while Norman foe in Hastings boasts."
The voice succumbed to death's swift call   105
and the youth's soul left mortal hall.
Elric embraced the lifeless child —
in grief renewed while rage surged wild.

All stood a while, in angst dismayed,
as in silence for that child prayed.   110
Till Leofwin from slumber urged
for them to rise as strength resurged:
"Come, let us go by wicked way.
Though grief-stricken we must away.
What is now left of this scant life,   115
let us avenge these hurts now rife.
And though the road lies long and bleak,
we must venture and King to seek;
beyond all hope England to save,
though our own lives lead to the grave.   120
No worse sorrow could we endure,
nor thought more fair our pain would cure,
than to be sure our folk stands strong
whose mighty deeds shall praise in song.
Long foreseen doom was so proclaimed   125
by God's Herald, who us had named,
when all our fates did now intend
for us to face a bitter end.
Whither shall we, of hope bereft,

guide weary feet through what lies left? 130
Whither roams death, eagerly sought,
as in foe's net our doom was caught?"
And as he spoke these words forlorn,
a few dark clouds were gently shorn.
As if to ease Leofwin's doubt 135
a slender ray of light did sprout.
Hallowed and bright it clove the air
and with intent shadows laid bare.
It fell on earth behind the hill
and on scorched fields its warmth did spill. 140
It shone briefly and grief did smite,
ere more dark clouds stifled that light.
Yet Saxons looked up to the skies
and tears of awe cleansed their sore eyes.

In swift earnest the Saxon lord 145
called them to haste, and on toward
he led them forth through the last stage
to quench war's lust, and angst assuage.
The ruined town they left behind,
and though the gloom did leave them blind, 150
they knew whence lay England's last stand
by divine sign which graced the land.
On a sudden they reached a vale
where darkness turned to shadows pale.
Towards the south rose steady slope; 155
a lonely hill where flocked all hope.

Most of its crown was wooded thick
with withered trees now bent and sick.
With shoulders bare, on hill battered,
there swayed the shapes of host gathered.   160

And thus by noon they crossed a stream;
swift Santlache[2], with its dimmed gleam.
That hill it flanked and scorched grass licked,
ere to the sea its course thus picked.
As shadows cleared they did descry   165
the King's banners against the sky.
The white wyvern fluttered in pride
on crimson field of flags thus dyed.
The two deep ranks of infantry,
where stood housecarls with fyrdmen free,   170
along the hill their thin lines drew;
each end thus flanked by trees not few.

Behind this stout resistance laid,
of weary men from long march frayed,
on horse sat he, King Harold nigh;   175
his stern face set, his sword held high.
On fatigued men his gaze rested.
Their armour rent, their shields tested.
The eight thousand now gathered there,
to the hill's foot they all did stare.   180
As the ground groaned from upheaval,
and swift succumbed to spells evil,

a cloud of dust rose down below
and thus approached Harold's own woe.
The braying horns in strangled light   185
revealed the ranks of Norman might.
Like hellish hounds that discord howled,
while mortal men to such noise growled.

As the dust cleared, Harold's men gazed
at wicked hosts who lands had razed.   190
Still hearts were eased, though hope was bleak,
in that tumult above the reek.
As wrath lessened lust stronger grew.
For they rejoiced as battle drew.
In his own mind each Saxon wished   195
a hill of slain with foes vanquished.
Their hearts grew hot and minds did crave,
from conquest dire England to save.
For Norman blood their swords did thirst.
Death-eager spears stout armour cursed.   200

Yet now there rode men of renown.
Their deeds of fame all else did drown.
For in their land across the waves
their folk praised them as gods by slaves.
Among thousands of footmen rough,   205
with pointed helms and chainmail tough,
who kite-like shields and bright swords bore,
there rode ahead these knights of war.

Most regal guard, more glances keen
than mortal man had ever seen.   210
By England's shores tales did profess
of their unmatched battle prowess.

On one great horse sat a man aged.
Through slender mouth he grinned, enraged.
The Duke's banner aloft he bore —   215
two fierce lions on field of gore[3].
Beside Eustace[4], a bishop[5] rode,
of whom tales tell no mercy showed.
Though man of God he claimed he was,
the mace he bore much death did cause.   220
As horns still blew without much rest,
a voice arose brimming with jest.
The Duke's minstrel, young Taillefer,
the *Chanson*[6] sang — rage did incur.
Meanwhile his sword he swung with ease.   225
The air it clove through stifling breeze.
His own men cheered at skilful play
while his deft grasp brought sword at bay.
Behind him rode, with young knight's grin,
Robert[7] the kind, the Duke's cousin.   230
In youthful age his fame had spread.
As men's captain he onwards led.
These knights now urged their army forth
to the hill's foot, towards the north.
There rode behind their Duke in ire: 235

his presence there, men did inspire.
Although a helm covered his face,
men knew their lord by stallion's grace.
The rider sat, glorious and proud.
The bastard[8] duke from whom most cowed.   240
He soon beheld a swift sword swing,
as gaze he bent on England's King.
He smiled grimly, his eyes aflame;
while thoughts arose of crown to claim.

Illicit birth caused much uproar   245
among nobles who sought to soar.
Yet through cunning he rose in might
and dukedom seized as his birthright.
He struggled hard. Normandy reigned,
and though still young much power gained.   250
His marriage[9] too thus swift assured
Flanders in war — allies secured.
When rumours reached the Duke in pride,
that King Edward[10] childless had died,
he sought to claim England's throne blessed.   255
Yet Godwin's son his hopes would wrest.
Treason! he claimed in his false thought.
Cruel vengeance eager he sought.
Councils summoned — grievance redress.
The cogent Duke strife did profess.   260
War was declared and conquest schemed.
Knights soon rode forth and army teemed.

The large fleet sailed, the seas did skim,
and massed the fields with thousands grim.

Upon the western flank was seen,   265
among archers and longswords mean,
silent while wrapped in mist of flame
Alan ar Rouz[11] — the Red Knight's name.
Less praise he earned, of virtue shorn;
while rumours spread of his vile scorn.   270
His lord he served with loyalty,
yet his mind craved for death to see.
With scarlet beard and crimson mail,
Bretons he led[12] through murky veil.
No helm he wore, nor shield he strapped,   275
yet single sword sheathed he kept.
He clutched the reins and tight he held.
Wisps of dark smoke from his hands swelled.
The horse he had sternly enslaved —
no other beast him could have braved.   280

Now as their foes' ranks were arrayed,
archers were sent up the hill's glade;
where Saxons stood, silent waiting
for sword's signal by Harold King.
With faithful kin, Leofwin lord,   285
gladdened by sight of their King's sword,
towards the hill eager he pressed
and hastened forth to reach its crest.

Yet as they went their course was stayed
by horseman few who them thus bade　　　　290
to lay down arms and state each name
ere false words flew and their lives claim:
"Whereto thou flee O strangers rife?
Where art thou bound in land of strife?
No travellers in war are there,　　　　295
but friends or foes who battles share."
Their voices quailed those riders terse
and with much dread their fates did curse,
to look upon such warriors stout
and thwart their way with hearts of doubt.　　　　300
In much concern to the hill's crest
they gazed in angst as their time pressed,
and all the while they held each spear
at Saxon kin while struck with fear.

The Saxon lord, weary in haste,　　　　305
stepping forth swift the speaker faced:
"Such kin that stands before you here,
by King's decree our ways drew near.
With these brave folk, England's finest,
I Leofwin return from quest.　　　　310
All those who now defy our foes
will do much well not to oppose."
With strength of voice flowed words of might
that horsemen quailed in great delight.
Their liege they led upon the hill　　　　315

where the King stood, silent and still.
Hear! the voices of armed men brave
while Harold King his greeting gave.
As Leofwin from deeds returned,
in songs they burst as hearts fierce burned.   320
While both brothers each other met,
the eldest spoke in earnest fret:
"Most glad am I to see you well
at the world's end where now reigns hell.
In haste we marched to meet fresh foes,   325
once you we left in the Weald's throes.
Though wearied much by battle fought
and long journey, the end we sought
to rally here as a last hope
by England's shores upon this slope.   330
But though we came from London¹³ swift,
with spirits high by God's own gift,
with strong intent to purge once more
our lands from dread while war did soar,
our southward march was stayed by doom   335
as fierce fire fell and death did loom.
A potent force marred our green earth
as the dark Duke approached in mirth.
For with him rides one praised in fear —
a red knight vile, who now moves near.   340
There! slithering amid the host.
William's champion flits as a ghost.
These spells he casts, at our hearts grope.

His presence here lessens our hope."
Silent then fell the somber King, 345
who at bold thought still dared to cling.
While at his kin and army bleak
in pity gazed, once more did speak:
"I see one less returns with you.
What went awry when fate thou drew? 350
Your sword you miss, that heirloom great.
Your scabbard rots without blade's weight .
Be swift and tell what tale of strife
shadowed your quest to seek thy wife?
Sorrow and grief lie in each breast 355
of those who dared the Weald to test."
So spake the King in awe at kin,
to see still stand bold Leofwin.
His eyes still shone with strength concealed
though much anguish his words revealed. 360
"Death and despair have guided me,"
Leofwin grim, with voice spoke free.
"Much grief endured by forlorn path
has filled our hearts with unquenched wrath.
Though great evil is now no more, 365
by courage found and oaths we swore,
my life suffered a grievous blow
for a great loss I now bestow."

As pity swelled, King's chest did fill.
Yet wistful words hardened his will. 370

Lust grew firmer, strength the stronger
to gain glory and battle conquer.
"We shall redress sorrows endured
and treat our wounds by win assured,
purging our land from Norman slaves   375
who now advance on hill in waves.
Come! Let us strike and swift drive out
these squirming worms into a rout,
and let us earn eternal praise
by our people till end of days.   380
Come! I clear see their flaws revealed.
We shall strike them with housecarl's shield.
Thieves and cowards! Mortal heathens!
To me my kin! Kindle beacons!"
A frenzy surged in Harold's heart.   390
His voice rose high like some aimed dart,
above the ranks of fyrdmen tall
and housecarls true in firm shield wall:
"Death! Death to all!" he called once more.
"On this grim day of hopeless war,   395
each one of you, in God's own eyes,
shall claim triumph o'er foes' demise."

The brave Saxons, loud roared their cheers,
as the King's words dispelled their fears.
Beornræd and Elric too   400
picked up the call and arms they drew.
They joined the ranks with brave Algar

and Ashlea, whose voice rang far.
While reckless foe onwards advanced,
upon the hill where Death thus danced.   405
Meanwhile Hrodulf, that man of God,
stood by Algar and at spear clawed.
In his drained mind terror lurked still,
though his spirit strengthened its will.

Leofwin stood amid their cries,   410
silent in thought, and with his eyes
beheld the strength of Norman host
as swift it swelled in its vile boast.
A chill crept deep as heart wavered.
His limbs stiffened, his mind faltered.   415
And all the while Harold, much crazed,
rallied his men whom their King praised.

He stood beside Wulfric the Tame,
one young in years who shunned his name.
The King's banner he held aloft.   420
Pale-faced with fear, his heart was soft.
"Let us hasten to the front line
and drive a wedge through worthless swine.
Thus together England we lead
to a new day," the King decreed.   425
"Nay, dear brother. I ask of thee:
do you not see thy own frailty?
Let not thy pride lead you astray,

as did my own blindness betray.
I see the strength of the Duke's ken[14],   430
and weariness that plagues our men.
I urge you swift to leave this place
and seek strong walls in which to brace.
There are warriors in Norman hosts
whose own prowess and hard-earned boasts   435
are of more worth than a ten score[15]
of those Saxons now at the fore.
I see their wrath and thirst for death.
Their voices howl with devils' breath.
I fear our shields will break once thrust,   440
like fallen leaves shrivelled by gust."
The King wavered at words of doom,
yet stood steadfast in crushing gloom:
"Nay! After such a dark road flowed.
We face our foes here, now, unbowed."   445

On a sudden a voice called out
of dread warning in shuddered shout.
A dark rain soared through gloomy skies
and fell down harsh on Saxon prize.
Shattering shrieks of shafts shrilling,   450
fell fierce in flight, on ranks spilling.
Countless arrows whistled through fields.
The sharpened points pierced deep in shields.
Struggling in flight to soar the air
over the hill through toxic glare,   455

more than a few fell down harmless,
but thousands plunged with eager press.
The Saxon wall, its structure held,
from harsh assault though shields were felled.
Norman archers loosed deadly swarm
of sharpened darts in ceaseless storm.
Some hapless shafts, misguided soared,
sliding through cracks and thus men bored.
Sharp screams rose shrill from shield wall set,
as Saxons bled and their deaths met.
With Wulfric too, the End was bound,
as down his throat an arrow drowned.
While Harold King and Leofwin
sought swift refuge with housecarl kin.
"Battle begins! Grab axe plundered!"
thus laughed the King, while darts thundered
above their heads. "Now Time us hails
to earn our place in England's tales."
Such lust lurked deep in Harold's eyes,
of deeds calling to lasting prize.
"Hold fast, stand firm! Sons of England!"
thus roared his voice to all at hand.

Yet Leofwin, bereft of speech,
to slain Wulfric his gaze did reach.
No life remained in those young eyes;
their light now spent by glory's lies.
That Saxon lord wept in his heart

460

465

470

475

480

at lives snatched swift by Norman dart.
And as his sight fell on stained field,
Leofwin knew their fates were sealed.   485
His thoughts fled far from that bloodshed.
Of Gyrth he thought, his brother dead;
from mortal world taken too soon
by Norseman's strength, cruelly hewn.
Of Eoforhild, that warrior strong,   490
who in life sought no man to wrong.
His soul was dragged through darkness deep
by evil sprites where shadows creep.
On Elvyn fair his thought dwelt last.
All hope he had was now long passed.   495
He knew no life beyond that field
of battle where his life would yield.
"This day's outcome let God decide.
Yet with England he shall sure side.
Firmer the will, stronger our might."   500
Harold's voice rose, raucous and bright.
The King smiled back at Leofwin.
Then from behind the shield wall thin,
he raised his hand and signal gave.
Battle began by England's brave.   505

Canto VI

No arrow flew. No dart did smite.
A silence reigned in waning light.
The shield wall stood from end to end
when a loud roar silence did rend.
Such shouts arose with voices shrill   5
as footmen charged upon the hill.
Kite shields glittered 'neath cloudy gloom
and boots thundered with thread of doom.
From Saxon line rained down in cheers
such sharpened shafts and fatal spears   10
upon their foes — that deadly hail,
its piercing claws keen did impale.
The grass turned red, the earth was stained.
Silence was breached by Normans pained.
Yet still the swarm of thousands strong   15
trudged up the hill to Saxon throng.
Harold looked on at hopeless sight
and urged his men to aim each flight.
While soaring wave of mailed men grim,
still roared forward with strength in limb.   20

Leofwin gazed at shields high-walled,
as wicked wave of foes was stalled.
While arrows sped and axes felled

his own axe grasped and shield he held.
Yet mightier proved Norman will   25
on that ill day, on Senlac Hill.
With tired limbs and blood-stained mail
thousands still trudged through mortal hail.
Against their foes their shields they rammed
and thrust their spears, and swords stern slammed.   30
Harsh rose the clash of blood-soaked brawl,
as bitter blades at flesh did maul.
The roar of war was deafening.
The cries of death were sickening.
Much blood was spilled as both sides met   35
yet Saxon wall withstood the threat.
Crimson clouds burst. Sweltered mists spewed.
Deep grunts and groans by hundreds hewed
left their frail breaths as eyes darkened —
dying voices strayed in the wind.   40

The Saxon line steadfast thus held.
In dreadful clash, savage strokes quelled.
Men strove wildly and skulls did cleave.
For fallen friends each man would grieve.
In their midst fought Harold the king   45
who bore his sword with mighty swing.
Nægling's keen bite relished in blood
of fallen foe that flowed in flood.
Golden it shone in gathered dark,
kindling Harold with fevered spark.   50

England's brave king swirling among
the raging foes, sword deftly swung.
Close by his lord Leofwin stayed.
With axe and shield on Normans preyed.
Many a foe he struck down swift,   55
and urged those thegns forward through rift.
They stemmed the surge of endless tide,
till its brute strength soon did subside.
Scarlet rivers slithered downhill
to wrathful Duke who cursed such ill.   60

But there upon a song arose —
a honeyed voice Saxon hearts froze.
A deep rumble, the earth sundered,
while cavalry onwards thundered.
That charge was led by one so named,   65
one Taillefer, in tales much famed.
The gasping dust from the scorched earth
rose in thick plumes amid his mirth.
Above the roar of gallops strained,
from faces brave much blood was drained.   70
Yet Saxon line, battered and frail,
stood firm once more to face the gale.
Within their ranks a voice soared high,
soft and graceful it did defy.
It firm opposed the Norman chant   75
which surged onwards bearing its brunt.
Forth stood she brave Ashlea strong.

Beside the King she sang her song,
as those voices battled in flight
while Saxon will dared Norman might.   80
Never was such a contest heard
of chanted hymns and spoken word.
No mortal ears will ever heed
such skill as those two foes in deed.
The neighing cries neared in earnest   85
towards the hill, upon its crest.
The Saxon wall with shields held high,
ardent now stood as charge surged nigh.

There was a man skilled with a spear —
Osgar by name who pride held dear.   90
He broke King Harold's firm decree
and from their shields he thus burst free.
At Taillefer, towards that knight,
he sprang across with keen shaft's flight.
At that minstrel his spear he aimed   95
with strength in limb and will inflamed.
Yet Taillefer, verse still sung clear,
and undeterred he shunned that spear.
In one fell swoop he swung his sword
and Osgar's neck he sheared as cord.   100

His song ended in bitter feud,
as horse met man and death ensued.
The clash of bones and riven cries

rose high above the din 'neath skies.
That wave of hoofs shattered the wall   105
and Saxons brave faced their downfall.
Still dauntless stood those who held fast,
though their brethren were flung and cast.
Leofwin struck his first horseman,
while Harold king with housecarls ran.   110
Those two brothers, fighting abreast,
against the tide their ranks they pressed.

Amid the fray, Ashlea strode
and with prowess her sword did goad,
as she battled that minstrel proud   115
upon his steed by clash uncowed[1].
That Norman bard, still chanting high,
withstood each blow aimed with a cry,
as Ashlea her sword swift drove
till one sure thrust his armour clove.   120
In sheer fury she sped in haste.
Round mighty steed she nimbly paced.
With sudden stab her keen blade hewed
through knight's sinew and voice subdued.
His song ended, his last breath fled,   125
as Taillefer hastily bled.
From his great horse he fell in gore
thus trampled on by seething war.

As battle raged and fates endured,

and no victor was yet assured,   130
Leofwin held the King's right flank
where Bretons surged and Saxons shrank.
Behind their ranks strode the Red Knight,
urging his men into fierce fight.
With great axes and unquenched ire   135
housecarls they slew, drowning in mire.
Alan ar Rouz with purposed aim
stomped forth thus grim — his eyes aflame.
With sheathed blade he towered high,
wading through men where fray lay nigh.   140
Saxons he grabbed in fervent thirst
and with bare hands their skulls he burst.
As withered leaves he snatched his foes
and flung them far as wild wind blows,
till shorn cries stole their final breath   145
and they plunged down to their grim death.
Akin a ship's own prow timbered,
carving the seas and waves splintered,
so forth that Knight clove through battle
while Saxons fled like ringed cattle.   150

The Breton flag — itself revealed —
with darkened bands on pallid field[2],
proudly it flew and men's will swelled
while hapless prey they boldly felled.
Leofwin roused those housecarls few,   155
kindling their hopes as axe did hew.

Yet terror lurked and swift did spread
as onwards came that Knight of dread.
The King's brother with wrath unfurled,
against those foes his resolve hurled.   160
The flag-bearer he struck with ease
as blood gushed keen from severed knees.
That banner tall swayed and floundered,
while men looked up — their stance wavered.
Doubt filled their minds at that fell sign;   165
their thoughts troubled by flag's decline.

Meanwhile that field, bloodied and crude,
prowess revealed in bitter feud.
Such great warriors on both sides dashed —
champions and lords, and fyrdmen clashed.   170
Leofwin heard a dying roar
as Elric fought midst gusts of gore.
To Eoforhild his thought now fled
where brother dear in dark lake bled.
With eyes awash in tears of pain,   175
he stabbed and slew as strength did wain
till grief-stricken heedless he rushed.
In thickest fray his cry was hushed.
Beornræd, amid fyrdmen —
with cudgel cruel from Glaistig's den —   180
each swordsman brave and noble knight
fierce in frenzy their souls did smite.
Beside him swung Algar's keen sword

in wild duel with Norman lord.
With feral skill his blade flesh ate,   185
where Sir Robert met his ill-fate.
With spear in hand, on left flank prayed
that frail Hrodulf whom to God bade
deliverance from that black day
ere wicked hosts the King should slay.   190

As a wild bear who's thus uncaged,
so there strode forth Odo enraged.
The bishop's mace crushed Saxon mail.
Each blow struck fierce with shriek and wail.
Before his eyes, through long dank hair   195
dampened by sweat and bloodied air,
he swift descried the Saxon priest
who slunk in fear as a trailed beast.
With arms outstretched no hurt he feared
as pride boasted and bile thus smeared.   200
In a loud voice from blackened beard
his harsh mouth screamed such words unfeared:[3]
"The Lord's own hand cradles my life,
safeguarding me from shaft and knife.
By divine right I slay thee all.   205
Let God's justice upon thee fall!"
With grimy hands his mace he seized
and in his mind was mighty pleased
to see Hrodulf cower in vain
ere smitten by that bishop's bane.   210

Yet deadly strike no flesh did sting,
nor bright mail struck or death did bring.
Light-limbed was she who priest did aid —
stout Ashlea that mace had stayed.

Thus battle swayed as day grew old   215
and the sea winds blew keen and cold.
Yet no sun pierced that choking gloom,
while Saxon host defied its doom.
As Breton flank faltered in fear,
and Leofwin drew housecarls near,   220
from the hill's crest their foes they thrust
with sword and spear into the dust.

Though tide had turned on that grim day,
and Saxons swept through dwindling fray,
Leofwin quailed and fates he cursed   225
as housecarls fey, bewitched by thirst,
ran down the hill in keen onslaught
as Bretons fled and safety sought.
None could restrain their fury's snare
while Saxon flank was thus laid bare.   230
"To me, to me! Steady King's men!"
Leofwin's voice raucous rose then,
as western flank broke off to slay
and Saxon line soon would give way.
Heedless of rout staunch thus remained   235
Alan ar Rouz whom no angst strained.

At housecarls few in shield wall's gash,
who still held back from reckless dash,
with purposed aim he strode within
and swiftly lunged at Leofwin.   240
His sword flashed forth. Sheer strength did wield.
The blade drove deep in that lord's shield.
That hallowed guard whose craft repelled
Glaistig's brute blow and Spear dispelled,
now clear it cracked as fractured wood —   245
though far was flung — force still withstood.
A deep gash crept round iron boss.
Riven timber slithered across.
Though shield did groan, sword's thrust deadened
and the Knight's grasp swiftly lessened.   250

While Saxon lord in trial thus strove
to ward brute blade as sharp it drove,
Harold's banner held the main line.
Wessex's wyvern golden did shine.
No hurt or wound troubled the King,   255
yet face was smeared with blood dripping.
His limbs he swung and iron rang
as foes succumbed to Nægling's fang.

Beyond the struggle there renewed,
blaring horns rang with voices shrewd —   260
moaning, wafting the fetid air.
Across clamour sudden did tear.

On stallion great with blazonry,
Duke William rode in fervent glee.
A golden crown on helm was shaped,   265
and chainmail thick his torso draped.
A mace he bore, iron-wrought death —
with single stroke, snatcher of breath.
Abreast, banner aloft was held
by bold Eustace whose pride swift swelled.   270
Behind Duke's steed, with lances keen,
thundered fresh knights with armour sheen.
Upon Harold and Saxons spent
with vengeful thirst their hatred bent.

Yet England's king was undaunted   275
as battle's lust him keen haunted.
Alone he stood, while housecarls lay
dead on the field in vicious fray.
Behind him came Ansgar the Old,
who staggered on with wounds untold.   280
The King's banner he held steadfast —
unstained it flew from stalwart mast.
Hundreds of men now took their place
beside their King, and terror face.

Their spears were set, their shields held proud, 285
and fyrdmen free rallied unbowed.
Horsemen thundered keen to assail —
their fury bent on Saxons frail.

Harold stepped forth. No helm he wore,
no armour stern his torso bore. 290
Nægling he thrust deep in the earth,
in England's soil — land of his birth.
From hallowed sword a quiver rent
the raucous air and banners bent.

A deep crevice before his feet 295
slithered agape by kingly feat.
Along the rift of seething ground
the Norman knights stumbled and drowned.
Into the mud horses neighed shrill.
Flung riders wailed and soon lay still. 300
On sharpened blades men were impaled
as fyrdmen thrust their spears unveiled.
The Duke's own steed floundered and fell
as William strove in slime to quell
the broken charge of knights who leaped 305
with heedless will on dead men heaped.
To those behind his voice he strained
— steeds to alight ere slaughter reigned.
Such tumult fierce drowned the Duke's call
while horsemen doomed faced mortal fall. 310
As disarray shook the Duke's line,
Harold did seize on fated sign
as lust for glory gripped his mind
and a false hope then made him blind.
"Onwards England! Now is the hour 315

when all tremble and foes cower.
Triumph shall soothe thy weary hands
and spurn this host to distant lands.
Each noble thegn and peasant's son,
eternal praise has justly won.   320
Now let your King lead you abreast
to reap glories by Heaven blessed."
The King of England, thereupon,
rushed into fray with sword keen drawn.
Upon the helpless knights he drove   325
his battle-lust, and deep he clove.
Behind him soared the strident roar
of Saxon wrath unfurled in war.
Axes and swords, and spears they snapped
upon champions and horsemen trapped.   330
Beornræd, soon at the fore,
sliced sure at him whom banner bore.
Eustace fell dead in bloodied mire
as Norman flag foundered in ire.
Slaughter ensued in gaping ground   335
where gallant knights death promptly found.

Then Duke William of Normandy,
amid the horror and the glee,
beheld a sight revealed in spite.
His fear-filled men fled from the fight   340
as rumour spread their lord was dead
and war was lost while blood was shed.

A mighty lord of people strong
the Saxon king had come headlong.
Behind him swept his loyal crowd,   345
keen to repel those forces cowed.
While battle soared and Harold leapt
in riven ground where marred men crept,
the Duke's horse fall thousands beheld —
from saddle's seat their lord was felled.   350
The worst they feared. Battle was lost.
That cruel day much lives had cost.
The cry spread far, *The Duke is dead!*[4]
as the main line splintered and fled.
The Breton flank and Flemish rear   355
in haste gave way — their spirits drear.
While disarray shook Norman host
William, unhelmed, aloud did boast:
"Attend! Attend! Your lord lives still!
Turn back traitors. Conquer the hill!"   360
His voice arose above the roar
of sure defeat that quells a war.

The Red Knight left his foe unslain
beneath his shield upon the plain,
and stormed across the battlefield   365
to aid his lord and triumph wield.
With severed guard Leofwin rose
in battered breath by smiting blows.
His weary heart by anguish stirred

at sight revealed and clamour heard.   370
His Saxon kin soared down the hill
in fevered lust and will to kill —
stalking their foes who fled in haste
far from the field as death they faced.
Wild-aimed arrows from archers fled   375
at Harold's men as pursuit led.
No few fell dead stricken by darts.
Others struck fear in Normans hearts.
"Reform the line! Defend the King!
This madness stay, to this hill cling.   380
Give up thy thirst for vengeance sought,
ere such folly brings all to nought. "
Leofwin's squall strayed far unheard
as the King's host poured out unstirred.
Yet all alone Harold soon faced   385
the Red Knight's wrath who forth now paced.

The clouds thickened and gloom deepened.
The sun westered, cold blew the wind.
England's own doom hung by a thread
as battle raged and men's lives bled.   390
Among the heaps of fallen friends,
and foes slaughtered to bitter ends,
the King's brother stumbled upon
the young cleric — from fight withdrawn.

There Hrodulf lay in slumbered swoon   395

beside corpses ruefully strewn.
His face was smeared with blood and dirt
while broken spear lay by unhurt.
"Awake young man! Ere 'tis too late.
Heed well these words and bear their fate.   400
Thy true purpose lies not in war —
nor with the knife or spear your bore.
Begone! and fly far from this field
to tell of deeds this day revealed.
Give hope to those whom comfort lack   405
amid plunder and reckless sack.
Unfurl the tale to England's sons,
to daughters dear and to loved ones,
of those who dared this doom defy
and to our foes our homes deny."   410
Hrodulf beheld his lord's keen glance.
With pity filled and noble stance,
a bloodstained hand his earl proffered
in sad farewell while leave conferred.
Tear-eyed Hrodulf, heeding his lord,   415
staggered away, and on toward
the north his will would find a way
to tell England of that sad day.

Harold ensued in bitter feud
against a foe with sword oft shrewd.   420
At his rival the Red Knight leapt —
with fell intent his own blade swept.

The King did prove, on that ill day,
his spirit's strength and skilled display,
which well befits a people's lord   425
who rules with heart and wields the sword.
Many a stroke was aimed with grit,
yet armour tough failed to submit.
As fate decreed it caused the King
to lose his step and firm footing.   430

Sunset weakened. The wind keen howled
to scatter far the airs much fouled.
Word that the Duke yet lived unbowed,
to quailing men courage endowed.
Battle-fervour resurged anew   435
as Norman host in boldness grew.
Cruel tides had turned, and Saxon hunt
soon fled the field from slaughter's brunt.

From rash bowman, a stray arrow
fell deadly swift amid such woe   440
to pierce Harold in his left eye[5],
who stumbled forth in searing cry.
Aimless Nægling thus smote the air,
while wicked foe laughed at despair.
The blinded King staggered and wailed,   445
with bloodied eye and senses veiled.
Rumour swept swift: *The King is dead!*
Stricken Saxons in haste far spread.

Behind their Duke the Normans swelled
up the sheer hill — by zeal impelled.   450
Leofwin ran to the King's aid.
His heart rippled as black grief weighed.
Alan ar Rouz, with fell intent,
to end kingship his will was bent.
Ere mortal blow pierced Harold's chest,   455
far in the ground Nægling he pressed.
Deep down it plunged from point to guard
till pommel gilt caressed grass charred.

Unfettered force scattered forthwith
from hallowed blade renowned in myth.   460
A gust of wind flung back that knight,
while the Duke's host with strength did smite.
Swordsmen and counts were beaten down
and Norman lords of such renown,
struck hard as stone by unseen blast,   465
were left startled and much aghast.
Encased in stone, the scalding blade
a thousand years would cling thus laid.
King Harold fell onto his knees
till ailing strength his limbs did seize.   470
Alan ar Rouz regained his stance.
With sword gripped tight, wrathful he pranced
at dying King to quell his breath
and quench his thirst for wicked death.
Yet Leofwin denied that prize   475

and rushed to face his own demise.
That dreadful clash commenced anew —
for the last time at each they flew.

The Saxon flanks, by Normans snared,
withered to nought — no soul was spared.   480
Though Leofwin with skill fought well,
no prowess great his foe could quell.
In weariness he struggled hard.
In fleeting breath he dropped his guard.
Snake-sighted foe stabbed his sharp fang   485
through unveiled chest where keen heart sang.
Leofwin gasped in great torment
as knighted sword clove through unbent.
Alan grimaced in triumph gained
as keener delved the blade bloodstained.   490

There, in Death's claws, his mind was healed.
The Saxon lord to doom did yield.
His guard he struck onto the blade
that shattered both, and sword mislaid.
From crumbled shield white light did drain,   495
while Alan's sword fierce snapped in twain.
Shining wisps spewed and swift shrouded.
Round the Red Knight the light crowded.
He struggled long in wraithlike chain
while Leofwin, beset by pain,   500
to writhing foe his axe he brought.

From high it swung and vengeance sought.
The cheek[6] was stained by bloodied neck.
No armour firm could stand such peck.
Alan ar Rouz met that praised end.   505
To Hell his shade swift did descend.

The wisps perished. That lord went pale.
Alone he stood o'er blood-soaked trail.
Strength ebbed away in the cold breeze
as wounded heart weakened with ease.   510
Darkness settled. Light gently failed.
His eyes faltered, his sight was veiled.
The mind was dazed and senses reeled,
yet heart burnt hot at sight revealed.

Saxons were strewn on sodden soil.   515
Normans plundered — eager for spoil.
Many a fair and noble thegn
and free man lay wounded and slain.
Among thousands of life bereft,
there Leofwin beheld the theft   520
of kin and friend who nevermore
in mortal world would die in war.
Beside Algar, with stern thrust speared,
Beornræd with wounds lay smeared.
'Neath bishop's mace Ashlea fell   525
in darkness deep away from hell.
With waning strength Leofwin crawled

towards the King — on foul field sprawled.
From pierced eye spewed his life away
yet weakened speech then still held sway: 530
"Those ancient words now do ring true,
as wise men once proclaimed they knew;
that kings are made for honour great,
not for long life and serene fate.
Yet now I rue the day we set   535
from our own halls to quell this threat,
and meet our fates in battle marred,
to yield England devoid of guard.
None shall now stem this endless tide
amid our doom and fallen pride.   540
God's own judgment has thus decreed
much woe and death for us who bleed.
Our lands lie prey to much pillage,
and folk from town and hushed village
shall be beset by wanton death.   545
We have lost all," trailed the King's breath.

Stillness settled on heaving breast,
as no more life coursed through his chest.
Harold's cold hand Leofwin held.
His own wound throbbed — at his will felled.   550
The King's brother, silent in grief,
upon the brink of life so brief,
uttered apt words towards the end
as failing breath his voice did lend:

"This day's brave deeds shall live in song.   555
Our people live, their will is strong.
Though darkness long shall veil these shores
much will endure in looming wars.
In time shall rise from shadows' shroud
an England free — proud and unbowed.   560
Whither our souls are bound to flee,
farewell brother. The King lies free!"

And thus as England fell from grace,
and blood ran down Leofwin's face,
his breath faltered — heart fell at ease —   565
no quiver stemmed the bitter breeze.

Epilogue

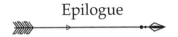

Silence fell deep. Nothingness stirred.
Life now did spring. Death thus interred.
Beyond the reach of mortal shores
there lay that place of peace from wars,
where Saxon lord tranquil sat still   5
by the old man of purest will.

Leofwin sighed. With voice broken
by sorrows deep words were spoken:
"In life I sought to bear my name
among the kings of renowned fame.   10
To make of worth my royal blood
and heave England from drowning flood.
My will strove hard to seek greatness
on battlefields where deeds impress.
My spirit burned with ardent need   15
to forge a way and history lead.
Though trials acclaimed and travels wide
bore me honour and much-sought pride,
I failed to see to my own heart
as Love was pierced by poisoned dart.   20
Zealous pursuit plucked me from home
to serve my King where foes did roam,
and chose a path awry to fate

that led me deep in the Weald's bait.
Ever-eager stubborn spirit   25
led me deeper to paths unlit,
till snared by lust and wicked sprite
was I hindered from my wife's plight.
Now here I am. England is lost.
My final quest my love has cost.   30
Burdened by sin at the world's end,
no words spoken can this wound mend.
I bear the pains I forged in life
where no Heaven can cleanse this strife.
No peace or rest does now remain   35
until my love I do regain."

That Saxon soul no more thus spoke,
but bent down sad till face did soak.
His eyes wept tears of bitterness —
no mortal voice could grief redress.   40
On shoulder hurt, a frail hand fell
as the old man sought pain to quell.
He smiled upon his grieving guest
then spoke fair words — heavenly-blest:
"From all burdens you are absolved.   45
No earthly strife, nor quest unsolved
need thou take heed. For Leofwin
I say to you as to thy kin,
that England's fate lies beyond you.
Thy famed prowess and strength you knew   50

has served thee well in life's sour test,
and now is time for deserved rest.
Rise! Glorious son of Hæstingas!
who swift in death have hastened thus.
You served England most just and fair,   55
but tides of Fate no man can bear.
In journeys long, seeking for pride,
you have grown much as glory died.
To fellow Man your kindness throve.
For loyalty you keenly strove.   60
Thy confession, to me just told,
is now needless in one so bold.
Through honesty thou have upheld
thy cleanest soul and grief have quelled.
True heart! Take heed! No sin nor grudge   65
shall mortal world against you judge.
No awry path or hapless quest
will keep thy soul from being blessed."

Leofwin felt his heart amend
once his sorrow came to an end.   70
He sighed deeply as thoughts he weighed,
while weariness swiftly did fade.
He rose renewed and on grass laid
his armour stained and axe decayed.
The fresh wind blew upon his face   75
while calm silence he did embrace.

As his time there began to wear,
that old man pure did thus declare:
"Turn weary face to sky's enchant.
Thy deepest wish fate does now grant."   80
Then Leofwin beheld a sight
at which in joy his heart did smite.
There stood his wife, Elvyn the fair,
who smiled in love and undimmed care.
There stood his love. No phantom sad.   85
To woman blessed, divinely clad,
he eager ran and keen embraced
as their great love by God was graced.

"Much have I prayed and long have yearned
to see thee safe and swift returned,   90
while you endured such loss and pain
that no man should ever again.
Well met my love, I see thee clear.
Beyond Death's fate now hold me near.
Now at world's end set yourself free   95
for in your hope you have found me."
Thus softly spoke the lady fair
as gentle breeze caressed her hair.
Her smile brought joy and boundless rest
to that brave lord at end of quest.   100
A light so pure shone in here eyes
akin the stars of nightly skies —
no ray of sun nor moon's bright sheen,

but undimmed light from Heaven keen.
By those two strode the old man's tread,   105
as tattered clothes and frail age shed
to stand unveiled in undimmed might
of God's glory all robed in white.
"What name be yours my fellow friend
who comfort gave me at the end?"   110
said Leofwin amid his tears.
His wife he clasped — rid of all fears.
Ere he faded in Flame sublime,
the angel spoke one final time:
"Call me Micel. Remember plain,   115
for both our paths now meet again."
God's herald bid its guests farewell —
at its ascent deep silence fell.
As a bright flash of searing light
it soared up high in divine flight.   120

And thus it was, lady and lord
with hands clasped firm did walk toward
the hallowed bridge and crossed with ease
where frail flesh fades in fragile breeze.
Towards Heaven both souls arose.   125
In God's bright realm they found repose
and bore with them their love unfurled
beyond the bounds of mortal world.

Notes

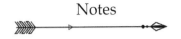

Prologue

1. An Anglo-Saxon tribe established between the 8th and 9th centuries.
2. Deprived of a helmet.
3. Awake.
4. Æthelred the Unready (King of England from 978 to 1013).
5. Witena ġemot, an Anglo-Saxon assembly of advisers to the king.
6. Edward the Confessor - King of England from 1042 to 1066.

Canto I

1. Morcar of Northumbria and Eadwine of Mercia.
2. Battle of Fulford (20 September 1066), which led to York's conquest.
3. Harald became a mercenary and commander in Kievan Rus' and the Varangian Guard in the Byzantine Empire.
4. Magnus the Good, King of Denmark and Norway. Succeeded by Harald as King of Norway in 1047.
5. Denmark.
6. Earl of Northumbria and Earl of Mercia defeated at Fulford.
7. Scandinavian name for York.
8. The River Derwent to the east of York.
9. The Battle of Stamford Bridge took place on 25 September, 1066.
10. William the Conqueror.
11. Halley's comet seen in March 1066.
12. The fall of the Roman Empire.
13. Legendary king of the Hæstingas tribe.
14. A legendary master blacksmith.
15. Old English for "blade of grass".
16. Old English for "fire edge"; *fyr* = "fire", *ecg* = "edge".
17. A sword used by Beowulf in the Anglo-Saxon epic poem.
18. Old English for "East Saxons" where the name Essex originates.
19. The Wyvern of Wessex - the emblem of Earl Godwin and his sons.
20. Archbishop of Canterbury and advisor to both Anglo-Saxon and Norman dynasties.
21. Protection or guard.
22. Anglo-Saxon shields were made of alder, birch, ash, poplar, willow and oak.
23. Old English for "shield".
24. The sun setting in the west.
25. English militia. Usually consisting of land workers.

Canto II
1. Courage.
2. At the Battle of Stamford Bridge, King Harold's men approached from the western side of the River Derwent, whilst Harald Hardrada's forces were camped across it to the east.
3. A large man or young giant.
4. Old English for "fated to die soon".
5. Old Norse for "Land-waster". In the *Heimskringla*, it was prophesied by Harald to bring victory to whoever bore it into battle.
6. South-west of Stamford Bridge where Hardrada kept his reinforcements.
7. Paul and Erlend Thorfinnson — Earls of Orkney.
8. Not fearful, showing courage.
9. Without shame.
10. A Norwegian noble, husband to King Harald's daughter.
11. In Norse mythology, Hel was the name of the Underworld for those who did not die a heroic death in battle.
12. The famed hall ruled by Odin where worthy warriors went to after a glorious death in battle.
13. Harald Hardrada.
14. Not worthy.
15. Feeling of grief and distress.
16. Old English for "fire-spewing dragon".
17. A description of the dragon in the Old English epic, *Beowulf*.
18. Latin name for "George".
19. A type of dragon that appears in British and Norse Mythology.

Canto III
1. Old English term for "woodland". It also refers to the forested area situated in southeast England.
2. Present tense of the word "to mar", meaning "to damage".
3. A spirit or ghost.
4. Mythical monstrous black dog from Northern English folklore.
5. Old English for "demon" or "goblin". Nowadays used in the context of a bad dream or nightmare.
6. A fairy.

Canto IV
1. To wash.
2. A supernatural being, spirit or ghost.
3. Deadly.
4. Protect.
5. Volcanic glass.

6. Known as Alan Rufus (or Alan ar Rouz). A relative of Duke William.
7. Old English for "Michael".

Canto V

1. Situated a mile north from where the Battle of Hastings took place.
2. A stream which flowed close to Senlac Hill where King Harold's forces were arrayed for the battle.
3. William II's coat of arms: two lions on a red background.
4. Eustace II, Count of Boulogne.
5. Odo of Bayeux, William II's brother.
6. Taillefer – an obscure figure said to have sung the *Chanson de Roland* to taunt the English during the battle, whilst juggling his sword.
7. Robert de Beaumont, 1st Earl of Leicester.
8. Duke William was also known as the Bastard. He was the son of the unmarried Robert I, Duke of Normandy, and his mistress.
9. To Matilda of Flanders.
10. Edward the Confessor was King of England before Harold Godwinson claimed the throne.
11. Breton for "Alan Rufus" or "Alan the Red".
12. Alan ar Rouz is said to have led the Breton force at the Battle of Hastings.
13. On his march south from the Battle of Stamford Bridge, Harold stopped in London to muster more forces before facing William.
14. Knowledge, awareness.
15. A score is a set of twenty.

Canto VI

1. Courageous, not frightened.
2. The flag of Brittany known as *Gwenn-ha-du*, "white and black".
3. Dauntless.
4. In the Bayeux Tapestry, William is depicted lifting his helm during the battle to prove he is still alive.
5. The Bayeux Tapestry depicts Harold with an arrow through his eye. Several chroniclers seem to sustain this theory. Yet, it is still debatable whether the figure in the Tapestry is hit with an arrow or is in fact holding a spear to be thrown at the enemy. Needless to say, the idea of King Harold being slain by an arrow has remained a powerful image.
6. The axe-side or cheek forms part of the axe-head.

Index of Names

Alan ar Rouz   The Red Knight, under Duke William.

Alfgar   Brother of King Harold of England.

Algar   Companion of Leofwin.

Ansgar   Harold's banner bearer after Wulfric's death.

Ashlea   Companion of Leofwin, sister of Eoforhild and Elric.

Beornræd   Companion of Leofwin.

Cnut the Great   King of Denmark.

Edgiva   Sister of King Harold of England.

Edith   Sister of King Harold and wife of King Edward.

Edward   King of England.

Edwin   Earl of Mercia.

Elric   Companion of Leofwin, brother of Eoforhild and Ashlea.

Elvyn   Wife of Leofwin Godwinson.

Eoforhild   Companion of Leofwin, brother of Elric.

Erlend Thorfinnson   Earl of Orkney, brother of Paul.

Eustace II   Count of Boulogne.

Frírek   Banner carrier to King Harald Hardrada.

Fyrecg   Leofwin Godwinson's sword.

Gærscíð   Gyrth Godwinson's sword.

Glaistig   The woodland fay of the Weald.

Godwin   Earl of Wessex, father of Harold, Leofwin and Gyrth.

Gunhilda   Sister of King Harold of England.

Gyrth   Brother of King Harold of England.

Harald Hardrada   King of Norway.

Harold Godwinson   King of England.

Hrodulf   Cleric, relic-bearer and companion of Leofwin.

Leofstan   One of the earls in King Harold's court.

Leofwin Godwinson   Son of Godwin of Wessex.

Micel   Archangel Michael.

Morcar   Earl of Northumbria.

Nægling   King Harold's sword.

Odo of Bayeux   Bishop and cousin of Duke William.

Osgar   Saxon spearman who challenged Taillefer.

Paul Thorfinnson   Earl of Orkney, brother of Erlend.

Starkheart   King Hardrada's dragon.

Stigand   Archbishop of Canterbury.

Sweyn the Mad   Brother of King Harold of England.

Robert de Beaumont   1st Earl of Leicester.

Taillefer   Minstrel to Duke William.

Tostig   Brother of King Harold of England.

Watt   Legendary King of the Hastings tribe.

Wēland   Legendary blacksmith.

William II   Duke William of Normandy.

Wulfnoth   Brother of King Harold of England.

Wulfric the Tame   King Harold's banner bearer.

About the Author

James Moffett was not a particularly keen reader during his early childhood. This changed when, aged 10, he discovered a book about life during the Middle Ages. Since then, he has been absorbing all kinds of facts and histories, going as far back as the Roman era and as recent as the Victorian age.

During his brief writing career, he has published a collection of short stories and a stand-alone novel on the character of Sherlock Holmes, including short story submissions to two anthologies about the same literary character.

He also maintains an online blog on the life and works of J.R.R. Tolkien: **atolkienistperspective.wordpress.com**

In his spare time, James engages in copious amounts of reading, tea drinking, and practising archery.

Printed in Great Britain
by Amazon